BY LOVE BEWITCHED

Whilst at art college in London, Laura had met Omar, an Arab medical student. When he proposed marriage, Laura knew she should have turned him down but she hadn't wanted to hurt him. Immediately after the wedding, Omar had had to return to Tripoli because his mother had been taken ill. Then tragedy struck. When Omar was badly injured in a car crash, his cousin, Ahmed, came to escort Laura to Libya. But why was this handsome young man so offhanded with her?

MOLLY LILLIS

BY LOVE BEWITCHED

Complete and Unabridged

LINFORD
Leicester

First published in Great Britain in 1981 by
Robert Hale Limited
London

First Linford Edition
published 1997
by arrangement with
Robert Hale Limited
London

British Library CIP Data

Lillis, Molly
   By love bewitched.—Large print ed.—
Linford romance library
   1. Love stories
   2. Large type books
   I. Title
   823.9'14 [F]

ISBN 0-7089-5174-0

Published by

F. A. Thorpe (Publishing) Ltd.
Anstey, Leicestershire

Set by Words & Graphics Ltd.
Anstey, Leicestershire
Printed and bound in Great Britain by
T. J. International Ltd., Padstow, Cornwall

This book is printed on acid-free paper

For Steve Hayes,
a man of the desert

1

IT gave Laura a breathless feeling as she looked up to find him staring at her. He in turn watched her moving across the blue mosaic tiles, his dark eyes expressionless behind the lowered web of his lashes. He was well aware that his surveillance disturbed her. He hadn't reached the age of thirty-four without knowing all there was to know about women. After all, he'd spent most of his adult years trying to keep clear of being tied to one or another of them.

What was there about this girl that made her different from the others? Why should she evoke a tenderness in him that he'd never known before? It wasn't that she invited tenderness. In the short time they'd known each other he'd found her self-willed; hard, even, and definitely not the broken-hearted

1

girl he'd expected her to be.

"Are you feeling more rested?" he greeted her as she drew nearer to the wrought iron table, strategically placed to get the maximum amount of shade.

"Yes, thank you," she replied, sitting on the chair he pulled out for her.

"Well, in that case we must continue with our conversation of this morning." He reached for the tall, fluted-topped jug and poured iced lime juice into the two glasses that had been laid out in readiness. Passing one of them to her, his fingertips brushed briefly against hers. "Time is getting short," he said. "I should like to get everything settled before I leave later today."

Laura lifted the glass to her lips, the lime juice proving to be the perfect thirst quencher. "But there's nothing to settle, Ahmed." She hesitated a little over his name. "I've told you, until I'm tired of saying it, that I don't want any of Omar's money. All I do need is my passport so that I can go back home."

"Libya is your home now, Laura.

When you married my kinsman, you became part of the family."

Laura put the glass down onto the table, the ice cubes chinking against the lead-cut crystal.

"Might I just remind you that if I hadn't had to stay behind in London, waiting for a stupid visa, I would have been with Omar on that awful day. If I had been in the car with him on that occasion he wouldn't have driven so recklessly."

"If. If. What is there about that small word that gives it the power to torment. In the first place, Omar must have known that you would require a visa to enter Libya. He should have seen to it earlier."

He didn't have the time before we married," she interrupted him.

"There was no great haste for the marriage to take place, was there?" When she didn't answer, he continued, "You could have waited and married here in Tripoli. That is what the family expected, once they knew about you."

3

Laura lifted her head, pushing her sun-glasses up until they sat more comfortably on the narrow bridge of her nose.

"I don't care now what the family expected. It's finished. Over." She brushed her soft brown hair away from her face. "I'm sorry, believe me, for all the upset our hasty marriage must have caused. Now all I want to do is to be able to pick up the pieces of my life again."

She made as if to rise but his firm hand on her arm detained her.

"My parents are saddened by the events of the past weeks. Stay in peace with them for a while. Stay until I get back from Rome; then if you still want to leave, I will escort you back to London."

About to tell him that she was quite capable of going back alone, Laura decided to say nothing. After all, Ahmed Saheed wasn't the type of man one argued with. It would be better to keep quiet and then to make her way home once he'd left for Rome or wherever he was supposed to be going. Almost as if he read her thoughts he reminded her that he still had her passport.

"Without that in your possession, you wouldn't be able to get as far as the airport," he drawled, a harshness touching his well-defined mouth.

Brown eyes, tear washed until they seemed almost hazel, met the cool gaze levelled at her across the table.

"That isn't the way of it, Ahmed," she flashed. "I still have my British passport. Omah is dead now, so there is nothing to keep me here."

"You wouldn't be lonely here, Laura," he continued, as if he hadn't heard her. "There are plenty of cousins who constantly visit the villa. There is also the pool just by the rock gardens in which you can swim each day."

"Why should anyone want to swim in a pool when the sea is so close."

"The pool is more secluded. Better for you than the open beach," the deep voice informed her.

"Which just goes to show how little you know about me or my way of life." Laura lifted angry eyes. "I've been used to being able to please myself, swimming where I like. I haven't been brought up to spend my days being covered from head to toe in *baracan*, like the women of your country."

"Tradition dies hard in the Eastern part of the world," was the quiet reply. "But even you must have noticed that the Western style of dressing has already reached our shores."

Was he laughing at her, she wondered, trying to fathom the look in the eyes levelled across at her. His features were stronger than Omar's had been. His face was hawklike in profile, with a hard, fierce look about it — quite different from the classical good looks his younger brother had possessed.

"It seems we shall have rain before much longer." Ahmed lifted his head to look up at the darkening sky. "But such storms pass swiftly at this time of the

6

year. You'll soon get used to the climatic changes." He gave her the benefit of one of his rare smiles.

"I've no intention of being here long enough to get used to anything," she replied defiantly. "It will be kinder to your parents if I leave here as soon as possible. To them I am just the English girl who married their son against their will."

"That's not true," he tried to assure her. "They need to feel that they can comfort you. You are now their daughter. Besides, what if there is to be a child of your brief union with my brother?"

"There won't be a child. I can assure you of that," she replied. "You see . . ." she began, about to explain that she and Omar had never been lovers in that sense, either before or after their marriage. But the way his lips twisted as he looked her up and down in that precise instant had the power to stop the words from being uttered. It wasn't his damned business, anyway, she decided, meeting the look he gave her with equal disdain.

"Of course," he drawled. "For one brief moment I had forgotten the preventive measures many modern girls choose to take."

Laura got to her feet, her hand coming up towards his face as latent anger zig-zagged between them. Quick as a flash his fingers caught and held her wrist.

"That is another of those unsavoury habits that won't be tolerated here, especially by me," he snarled, letting go of her wrist.

"Why do you want to keep me here when you obviously dislike me so much?" she asked, feeling the first spots of the rain he'd forecast falling softly onto her head.

"My wishes do not count," he told her in his precise English. "I shall be leaving shortly, anyway."

"Well, don't expect to find me here when you get back." She started to walk towards the archways spanning the outer courtyard.

"I thought I'd made it clear that escape is impossible," he said, catching up with her.

"You're an arrogant bastard." She turned to face him. "But if I can't leave the country, it doesn't mean that I've got to stay here at the villa. I hate it here and what's more, I hate you."

By moving closer to her he forced her to step back until she rested against the sun warmed support of the wrought iron sundial. With hair-trigger alertness, strong fingers settled about her chin, forcing her to look up into the lean, dark hardness of his face.

"Keep on hating me, little one," he said, his voice a husky thread of sound. "Hate enough for the two of us. At least that should be better for you than not feeling anything at all."

With an abrupt movement he turned from her to stride away across the covered patio towards the furthest corner of the building. Laura passed no one as she walked slowly across to the wide marble stairway and up to where her rooms were situated. The views from the windows were delightful, but now Laura stared out without actually seeing the wild beauty of the rock garden below. Resting her forehead against the cool glass of the window she thought back to the events that preceeded her arrival at the home of the Saheed family.

She had first met Omar on the stairs of the tall, Victorian house in London's bedsitter-land. Her room had been on the second floor, Omar's on the one above. Laura, with the trained eye of the artist, had been fully aware of the fine eyes and good bone structure of the young Arab. He was studying medicine at the nearby teaching hospital, while she was in the final year at the art college. As the weeks passed into months, their friendship blossomed into something stronger. During those hot summer days she'd often wished that she had been as good at portraiture as she was at landscape painting. When

Omar had first mentioned an engagement between them, Laura had allowed herself to be swept along on the tide of his enthusiasm. It was good, she told herself, to have a steady boy friend, especially one as thoughtful and as good looking as the young Arab medical student. But Omar, impatient by nature, wasn't content to let the months unfold. He wanted marriage without undue delay. Almost before Laura knew it, he had applied to the Embassy and had seen to all the other legal requirements. The speed at which everything moved surprised her, especially as she had read somewhere that permission to marry outside one's own country was often a long drawn out affair. About that time, after his request had been granted, Omar had been summoned back to Tripoli because of his mother's sudden illness.

Laura knew she should have told Omar then that she didn't really want to marry him. Instead she'd offered to go back to the house to pack for him.

She'd felt so relieved at his impending departure, she hadn't been really interested in his assertion that it was all a trick on his mother's part to get him home to Tripoli before he had the chance of getting married to Laura. The remainder of his conversation on the afternoon that now seemed to be a million years ago had filled her with despair.

"One more day won't make any difference to my mother's health." His smile had been that of a conspiratorial youngster when he told her that they were to be married by special licence the following morning, and were to fly to Tripoli on the afternoon flight. "Tell me how wonderful you think I am for arranging everything so efficiently," he'd pleaded, his hands warm across her back, his dark eyes soft and appealing.

Laura had got as far as opening her mouth to explain how she really felt, but the words that had trembled on her tongue had never been uttered. Instead, she'd allowed him to think that she was as eager for the union as he was. She knew she could never hurt him. He was too good, too caring for that. She couldn't explain her actions either then or now. Perhaps her reasons had been purely selfish, knowing that he would love and cherish her always. She'd cared about him, in her way, from the beginning and with the hope that this feeling would strengthen with the years, she'd fallen in with the plans he'd made. Laura's friend, June, a fellow art student, and Osmand, a colleague of Omar's, had been the only witnesses at the brief, impersonal ceremony. They'd only had enough time afterwards to have a coffee together before Omar and Laura had picked up their luggage and caught the tube out to Heathrow. It wasn't until they'd reached the check-in point that Laura had been told that she wouldn't be allowed to enter Libya without the required Arabic visa in her passport.

Omar had wanted to postpone his

flight, but she had persuaded him to go without her, arranging at the same time to join him in Tripoli just as soon as the problem had been sorted out. Now Omar was dead, and Laura still felt guilty because of the light-hearted feeling she'd had as she watched the plane take off without her. Now that all seemed ages ago. She wondered, as she stood against the window, if that gentle tenderness that had existed between them would have been strong enough to carry them through a lifetime of being together. She'd enjoyed being kissed by him, caressed by him, but on those occasions when Omar would have taken things further, she'd always been the one to draw back. He had respected her wishes every time and in turn had praised her for her virtue. After Omar had gone back to Tripoli, she'd waited apprehensively for her visa. It was lonely without him and there had been a time, then, when she'd persuaded herself that all would be well between them once they were together again.

She'd been lucky enough to rent her old room again, but hadn't been able to get reinstated at the art college. It had been one of those days when soft fluffy clouds floated high in the sky when she'd gone off with a light heart to pick up her visa from the Embassy. With luck she could be in Libya by the end of the week; she'd smiled softly to herself, mounting the steps of the tall, Victorian house two at a time. It had been something of a shock to find Ahmed Saheed waiting there for her. Laura couldn't recall his exact words. All she remembered was that Omar had been injured in a car crash, and that the tall, arrogant stranger had come to take her to his bedside.

Laura hadn't been deceived by Ahmed Saheed's gentleness as he'd waited for her to pack. She was well aware of his silent censure, and wondered at the reason for it. Once they'd boarded the plane belonging to Libyan-Arab Airlines he had been a silent figure sitting beside her, speaking to her only on matters concerning her immediate comfort. Feeling very much in awe of this older brother of Omar's, she had answered him in monosyllables, wishing he'd sent a cable to her instead of coming to collect her. When the 'no smoking' and the 'fasten seat belts' signs were flashed on, Laura, usually a good traveller, had felt sick with tension. The aircraft started to descend, circling over the blue waters of the Mediterranean. Looking through the window beside her, she watched the waters of the harbour spread out beneath them. Ahmed chose that moment to tell her that pirates had once sailed from the harbour to plunder the vessels plying the middle seas.

Laura wasn't interested in hearing about the harbour or pirates. All she wanted then was to get to Omar's bedside as quickly as possible, thinking that as soon as Omar saw her there he would be set on the speedy road to recovery. There had been no cuts or gashes to mar the perfect features, and looking down at her young husband, lying so peacefully in the narrow hospital bed, Laura became faint with relief. She thought she'd felt him stir as she'd rested her lips against his cheek before the sister had ushered her from the room. Ten minutes later, when they'd told her that he'd died without regaining consciousness, Laura hadn't been able to take it all in. She'd refused to believe them. They, the medical staff, had made a mistake. Omar was just resting. It had been Ahmed who had made her go back into the side ward; Ahmed who had made her touch the waxen cheek, before he'd picked her up and carried her out to the waiting car.

At first, it was as if the family blamed her in some way for Omar's untimely death, but after the funeral it was considered to be Allah's will. Everything seemed to be settling down, life in the Saheed household carried on as usual.

Laura sighed as she pushed the window a little until it was open enough for her to look down onto the garden. The rain had stopped as suddenly as it had started. The air was filled with the sharp, sweet smell of the oranges growing in the citrus groves flanking the large, Moorish styled villa. From the minarets of innumerable mosques, the chanting of the Holy Men echoed across the city, calling the faithful to prayer. Five times each day, from sunrise to sunset, verses from the Koran were chanted from the minarets with the same precise regularity. In some strange way Laura began to find a measure of peace each time she listened to the sing-song call.

She was lucky, she supposed, in the fact that most of the Saheed family spoke good English; though there were times when the family congregated together for the evening meal when they usually conversed in Arabic. There was just the immediate family and two aged aunts who actually lived in the sprawling, beautiful villa, but each night the driveway seemed to be crowded with the cars of the many visitors.

Laura knew that another branch of the family lived at the nearest villa, four or five minutes walk away along the wide, sandy road. It was there that a number of the cousins lived, but although a couple of them were round about Laura's age, they treated her with frigid politeness. Only Suleiman, who had just completed his military service, bothered to draw her into the nightly conversations.

Perhaps part of the trouble was of her own making, Laura decided, after one such evening. Since her arrival in North Africa, she'd held herself aloof, not wanting to be drawn into the bosom of the family.

At that moment a gentle tapping on the door disturbed her jumbled thoughts. Opening the door she was surprised to find Omar's father standing there.

"My wife is worried about your lack

of appetite, hence this ladened tray."
He smiled, the pale olive skin crinkling
about his heavy-lidded eyes. "We both
decided that perhaps you would rather
eat your midday meal in the privacy of
your room."

"I think the unaccustomed heat
bothers me a little." Laura returned
his smile shyly. "It's a very kind
thought, though." She invited him into
the room, crossing over to make a
space on the table for the ovalshaped
silver tray.

"When you feel in the need for
company, you must come downstairs,"
the low pitched voice informed her.
"While you continue to close yourself
away, the others will respect your wish
to be alone. You are missing the best of
each day, daughter." He folded his
hands together after depositing the tray.
"After all," he continued, "there is
more to being a member of a family
than merely being together for the evening meal." He turned to walk away.
"Enjoy your lunch," he said kindly.

"*Shukran,*" Laura replied.

"*Afwan.*" He smiled over his shoulder. "It is my pleasure to serve you, daughter."

The door closed behind him and Laura looked down at the food set out in the individual china dishes. She didn't think that she'd get through the *Sharba,* the delicious soup that the family had most days, but in less than half an hour she'd finished the soup, and the chicken breasts in thick, creamy sauce. The fact that she had eaten and enjoyed the meal would please her mother-in-law, Laura decided. Perhaps if she took the empty tray down to the kitchen right away, there might be the possibility of finding Mrs Saheed there.

But only Mabrouka, one of the Egyptian servants, was there to take the tray from her. She was delighted to see that all the food had been eaten. "Mrs Saheed in the garden." She smiled, showing four gold teeth, pointing with a slender brown finger towards the back of the villa.

Making her way through the building, Laura pulled open the sliding door and stepped out into the heat of the large, beautifully tended garden. Standing uncertainly beside the fountain she saw that Omar's mother and his two elderly aunts were sitting together beneath the overhanging branches of a broad, leafy tree, while a young Arab girl swung to and fro on a swaying sun lounger. The girl was the first to greet Laura.

"*Ahlan-wa-sah-lan*," She smiled shyly, moving along the lounger to make room for Laura.

"Hello," Laura replied, moving slowly to join the group. If the other three had been slow in greeting her, the warmth of their smiles made up for it. The old aunts spoke only Arabic but even with her limited vocabulary, Laura knew that they were pleased that she had joined them. Omar's mother didn't speak English nearly as well as her husband did, but her manner was courteous and gentle as she introduced the doe-eyed girl to Laura. "This is Jameela," she said quietly, "the daughter of my oldest friend."

The girl's hand felt boneless as Laura's fingers closed over hers. "I am happy to meet you," the young girl said. "I wish your first visit here could have been a happier one for you."

Laura felt the other girl's sympathy.

"I wish that, too," she managed to reply.

Once the first moment of awkwardness had passed conversation soon began to flow freely between the two girls, much to the obvious delight of the others, who now seemed content just to watch and to listen. Jameela was interested in hearing all about the English way of life, wanting to know what Laura and other girls like her did for a living. She in turn told Laura about the country's feast customs, and about the school where she and her sister had studied.

Later, when the sun had moved across the sky, the two aunts got up from their chairs to scurry indoors, their dark coloured *baracans* wrapped closely around them. Shortly afterwards Jameela said that she must leave for home but would be back later with her parents.

"Drive carefully, Al-walad." Mrs Saheed bent to kiss the girl on both cheeks. "It has been good to see you today."

Jameela answered in Arabic before turning to say goodbye to Laura. Laura watched her walking away, her movements graceful in the long white garment she was wearing.

"I didn't realize that Jameela drove her own car." Laura turned to face her mother-in-law.

"Quite a number of the young girls of our country drive these days," the older woman replied, her eyes in that moment reminding Laura of Omar's.

Without prior thought she said, "Omar had your gentle beauty, Mrs Saheed. I wish I could have painted his portrait while I had the chance."

24

Noting the swift flicker of pain her words evoked, she apologized for her lack of thought.

"It is good to talk together even about sad things," she was told in reply.

In an effort to lighten the mood between them Laura asked about Jameela's work. "We didn't get round to discussing that." She smiled as they walked towards the villa.

"She works at one of the clinics but has been staying at the home of one of her aunts for a while." They had almost reached the open doorway when the older woman laid a detaining hand on Laura's arm.

"Ahmed said that you were not to be told." She hesitated for a second or two. "But I think it is best that you should know that Jameela is the girl who was betrothed to Omar. They had been promised to each other from childhood. Plans had been made for them to marry next year."

2

BECAUSE of what Omar's mother had told her, Laura felt even more ill at ease with the family. As the days passed she wondered how Jameela could be so friendly towards her. In similar circumstances she doubted very much if she would have been so cool about it all. Perhaps there was something in the other girl's make up that wasn't in hers, she decided. Even when she'd told Jameela how sorry she felt for the way things had turned out, Jameela merely smiled in that grave way of hers, and said that she could understand why Omar had fallen in love with Laura instead of her.

"I must have seemed quite a dull person when he compared me with you." She smiled without rancour. "But that is the way of things and life must go on."

Instead of setting Laura's mind at rest, Jameela's gentle acceptance of the situation only served to make her feel more up-tight. It would have been easier all round if Ahmed hadn't put her passport in a safe place. With her passport in her possession she could have been back home by now. He didn't seem to realize how important it was that she should get back there as soon as possible. The longer she was away, the harder it would be for her to find a job. She'd have to get some sort of a job to be able to live. Her grant, small though it had been, had stopped when she'd left the college. The rent of her room would be in arrears by now, and even though she'd always been a particular favourite of the landlady, she couldn't expect her to hold it for her indefinitely. Of course, there were lots of openings for girls with Laura's artistic flair, but her chances were slipping away day by day.

She wasn't exactly a prisoner at the villa, but being forced to stay there, at least until Ahmed's return from Rome, was proving to be irksome, to say the least. She felt bored and often ill at ease in this strange environment. Of all the people belonging to the large, closely knit family, she found Suleiman the easiest one to get on with. She was more than pleased when on the Friday morning he called at the villa to ask her if she'd like to drive into the city with him.

"Aren't you working today?" she asked, knowing that he had just been appointed to one of the Government departments.

"Today, being Friday, is our Sabbath, so I am free to show you a little of Tripoli," he said. "I think it is most important that you should be well-informed about past and present happenings in your new country."

Mr Saheed was delightful when Laura told him that Suleiman had invited her out for the day.

"Who better than Suleiman to take care of you," he said. "Enjoy yourself, daughter, and be certain to get him to show you the older part of the city."

Sitting beside Omar's cousin as he drove along the broad, tree-lined road, Laura looked out with wide, interested eyes.

"I'd never heard much about Tripoli until I met Omar," she turned to say to Suleiman. "All I really knew was that it is one of the main cities of Libya," she said.

"Don't tell me you didn't learn about the North African campaign of your country's second great war?" The young Libyan laughed. "I understood that the wars of your country are constantly referred to."

"Oh, they are," Laura agreed, "but I've never been interested enough to bother, except, of course, in an historical sense. Even then I'm more interested in ancient history."

"Oh, so you agree with the words of the great Cicero, 'History is the witness of the times, the torch of truth'," he said, stopping at the crossroads.

"It's different here from what I expected it to be," she said. "I imagined it would be more desert instead of all these modern buildings."

"I expect you thought we were all nomads living in tents and tending camels and goats." He stopped talking just long enough to point out the pink mosque with its two slender minarets against the skyline. "That way of life belongs to the old days, though there are of course still Bedouins who roam the desert, depending mostly on their meagre harvest for a living, and following the rains for suitable pastures for their modest herds of goats and camels."

"Do you ever go into the desert?" she asked. Suleiman shook his dark head.

"I thought I'd made it plain that I'm more interested in the workings of the city," he said. "Ahmed is the family's man of the desert, but that is because he lived there for the first fifteen years of his life."

"I don't understand you." She

shifted her position so that she could look at him, feeling a sudden interest in what he was about to tell her.

"Ahmed's father was a Bedouin of high intelligence. He studied the different kinds of soil and the rock formations of the regions. He was, how do you say it, a geologist?"

"Yes, I know what you mean. What about his wife, Ahmed's mother?" she asked. "Was she interested in his work?"

"Riad, Ahmed's father, met Medeleine, a talented French archaeologist, while she was in Libya working at the site of one of the Roman ruins."

"How romantic!" Laura gasped. "I bet that caused a bit of a stir."

"News of their marriage made the headlines of newspapers across the world. People still talk about it."

"Did the marriage last? Was her love strong enough to bridge the gap between East and West?"

"She loved him enough to share his tent, to ride beside him from the coastal zone to the mountains, across the forbidding desert and beyond. I never knew them, but in Ahmed their goodness lives on."

"So Ahmed isn't a Saheed, then," she murmured. "Yet he calls them Mother and Father, and they in turn treat him like a well loved son."

"Ahmed's father and Omar's father were cousins. When Ahmed's parents died from some obscure fever, it was only natural for the young orphan to join the family." He slowed down as the road narrowed, picking up speed again afterwards. "Did Omar not talk about us?" He smiled swiftly down at her.

"Not a lot," she replied, "except to tell me that you were all very close to each other, and that he adored every one of you, especially Ahmed, his elder brother."

"Does it hurt to speak about Omar?" he asked. "I find it hard to think of you as my cousin's widow."

"Perhaps that's because I don't wear

mourning clothes," she replied thoughtfully. "I grieve for him; of course I do. He was so beautiful, so young, but I feel the hurt more for his mother than for myself."

"Your unselfish thoughts do you credit," he said gently, his words dropping like salt into the open wound of her guilt.

Though the roads were congested with vehicles of all shapes and sizes, Suleiman still managed to keep up a steady flow of conversation. He was certainly keeping his word about educating her in every aspect of life in Libya, past and present.

"Greeks, Phoenicians, Romans, Vandals, Byzantines and the Turkish Ottomans have all had a hand in things," he told her as they reached the place where to park the car.

"You certainly know your subject," she said when he pulled up in the narrow side street.

"My country, past, present and future, is my favourite subject," he replied with a proud lift of his head as he got from the car and hurried round to let her out.

Laura walked beside him, her footsteps matching his on the cobblestones of the wide, sunlit square. Passing beneath a carved, ancient archway. Suleiman told her that they were now in the *souk*, the market place.

"What a fascinating place!" she said, looking up at the ancient carvings high on the weathered, greystone walls that enclosed the Aladdin's cave of tiny shops. Fine silver wear, heavily embroidered kaftans, tapestries worked in glowing colours, pottery from nearby Tunis, were displayed beside Westernized suits and dresses; beautifully made lace and leather goods. There were so many of the small shops to browse around, but Laura was tireless as she walked across the worn cobblestones, looking first in one shop and then the others. When it was time to go back to the place where they'd left the car, Suleiman suggested that Laura should go with him to pay a visit to some friends of his.

"You will like Ali and Jasmin. They married only recently and would be pleased for you to call upon them," he said, unlocking the door of the car for her.

Even though the car had been parked in the shade for most of the day, the interior felt hot and airless.

"It will feel cooler once we are on the move." Suleiman slid into the seat beside her.

He reached for his sunglasses from the compartment below the dash. "Before we set off, would you like something to eat; a cool drink perhaps?" he asked. "It will take us only a short time to get back to the restaurant where we had our meal earlier."

Laura assured him that she was neither hungry nor thirsty.

"I dare say my friends will expect us to share a meal with them," he replied, setting the car in motion.

The roads were even more congested than they had been earlier. When Laura remarked about this, Suleiman told her that it was usually much busier at this particular time of day.

"It is the hour when most of our people are in a hurry to get home after the day's work. It being Friday, though, many do not work. You have no need to worry about the busy state of the road," he said smiling. "I am a capable driver and the blaring of the others' horns does nothing to bother me."

"Perhaps I feel strange in the passenger seat because you all drive on the right-hand side of the road," she replied.

Laura commented on his perfect use of English. "You all have the same precise way of speaking."

"I expect if you were to learn to speak my language, you would no doubt be taught the standard Arabic which is often referred to as classical. Even this has undergone changes like any other modern language. New expressions and up-to-date words have been introduced so that the classical Arabic is kept abreast of the times."

Moving into the correct lane of the new dual carriage-way, Suleiman drew her attention to the modern suburb of Georgempopoli. A mile or so further on he turned right, into a quiet road, telling her as he pulled up in front of one of the white painted villas that his friends lived in the top section. "Their own villa is still being built," he said.

Ali and Jasmin were delighted to welcome them both and insisted, as Suleiman had said they would, that they should share their evening meal with them. Time passed swiftly, especially when they all became engrossed in watching an English film on the couple's newly acquired video set.

The sun had long since disappeared over the horizon by the time Laura and Suleiman left the comfortably furnished apartment. The few people still walking about were being enveloped in the swiftly descending dusk.

It was only when Suleiman drove the car up the dusty road to the villa that Laura remembered that the family were dining out that evening.

"Do you want me to come inside with you," Suleiman asked when he got out of the car to walk with her towards the house.

"No, thank you," she replied, fumbling in her bag for the key Mr Saheed had given to her that morning. "I think I shall have an early night."

Suleiman stared down at the pale blur of her face. "I have not tired you too much, have I?" he asked with swift concern.

"Not at all. I've enjoyed every minute of today," she said.

They shook hands gravely and he bent forward to kiss her gently on both cheeks.

She said good night to him and turned to push the key into the lock. The door swung open on well oiled hinges and seconds later she heard

Suleiman restart the car. A light had been left burning ready for her return, the low voltage bulb glowing softly through the orange tinted shade of the lamp at the far end of the wide entrance hall. The flowers that had been arranged in the tall terracotta urns only that morning were already drooping, their scarlet petals like drops of blood on the milky whiteness of the marble floor. Passing the urns, Laura bent to pick up a number of the velvety petals and turned to drop them into the oversized ashtray on the low, glass-topped table. Catching a slight movement from the corner of her eye she froze for a split second before turning her head to stare towards the arched moorish window. She took a gasping lung-full of air, her heart tripping in her breast at the sight of the tall figure silhouetted darkly against the moonlit recess.

"Have you had an enjoyable day with yet another of my young cousins?" the deep voice greeted her.

Laura's hand was still pressed against her throat where it had flown with the first shock of seeing him there. "You scared me half to death," she gasped as he moved to stand in front of her, looking very tall, very different in the full length cloak he was wearing over crisp white Arab robes. She was used to seeing him in well cut, Westernized suits which fitted perfectly across the breadth of his shoulders; but now, in his black cloak, he had the look of some splendid Mephistopheles.

"I asked you a question," he drawled, looking down at her from his superior height. "Perhaps you will answer me."

"Yes. Yes. I have had an excellent time," she snapped. "Now may I pass, please."

She tried to push past him but he moved closer, until he was near enough for her to feel the warmth of his breath against her forehead. Laura looked up into his face but the angry words she'd been about to say died in her throat.

Gold flecked brown eyes drowned in inky black as he stared down at her. She saw the muscle move in the smooth, lean cheek and watched his mouth tighten into a thin, hard line.

"What are you trying to prove?" His tone was gravel pitched.

"I don't know what you mean," she gasped, trying to lift her chin just a fraction higher than usual.

"Suleiman is too young for you to ensnare with your beauty. You will leave him alone, do you hear me?"

She swallowed painfully, the sound loud in the enveloping silence.

"What I do is no business of yours," she managed to say at last.

"But I intend to make it so, I can assure you," was the terse reply as he turned on his heel to leave her standing there.

Laura watched the tall figure moving away. What had he meant? What did he want from her?

She heard the door close behind him; seconds later a car engine roared into life and she knew that Ahmed had driven away from the villa.

The following morning she decided to speak to Omar's father. Surely he realized that she had no intention of making her home in Tripoli. She thought she'd made it clear from the beginning. She didn't have a residence permit, so they must all know that her stay could only be of a short duration. Making her way downstairs to the room where breakfast was usually served, Laura tapped on the door hoping to find her father-in-law eating alone. Pushing open the polished oak door, however, she found Ahmed sharing the first meal of the day with him. She stood hesitantly against the door, wishing suddenly that she hadn't been so impetuous. The older man looked up first, inviting her to join them, and in some undefinable way Laura knew that Ahmed had known she was there even before he'd turned his head.

"Come, daughter, will you have a glass of *chai* or do you prefer coffee?"

Her father-in-law pulled out the chair for her.

"Coffee, please," she replied, sinking down onto the low chair. She took the coffee he poured for her, noting as she did so that both men shared the preference for the hot, green tea.

"I suppose you miss your English style breakfasts," the older man remarked when she refused the scrambled eggs he offered her.

"Not at all," she smiled. "I never was a great lover of bacon, anyway."

He asked her then what her plans were for the day ahead. Without prior thought she told him that she would like to borrow one of the cars, if that was possible.

"I can drive you wherever you wish to go," Ahmed offered.

Laura turned her head to look at him. "I'd rather go alone," she replied stiffly, turning her attention back again to her father-in-law. "I had thought of driving out to Leptis Magna." She paused, meeting the hooded eyes of the older man.

"You would find the journey tedious, especially as you have never driven while you have been here. Better to allow Ahmed to drive you there," he suggested.

"It doesn't matter," Laura replied, aware that Ahmed was watching her with narrowed eyes. "Suleiman said he would take me sometime, but I thought this would be the best chance of going alone, perhaps taking my sketch pad with me."

"Ah. You wish to capture on paper the beauty of the city that was more or less buried for centuries beneath the encroaching sand."

Laura looked up in surprise. "You understand how I feel about art." She leaned forward to replace the half empty coffee cup onto the low table. "While I'm here in your country I would like to sketch some of the things I see here."

"While you are here?" The fine eyes looked from Laura to Ahmed and then back again. "But I thought it was arranged that you should make your home here with us. It is our duty to protect, to care for you."

"Leave it, father." Ahmed spoke gently but firmly. "I will speak to Laura again about our way of doing things."

Mr Saheed got to his feet. "Perhaps now will be the ideal time to tell her. I will leave you both in peace."

Laura watched him go from the room and then turned to face Ahmed again.

"There isn't anything to discuss. You already know my intentions to go back home. You know I'd kept my room on. You were there when I paid the advance rent. It's important that I should go back there as soon as possible."

"Perhaps there is some other man waiting there for you," he suggested with a coldness that sent the colour from her face.

"That is just the remark I would expect from you." She stared across at him with wide, angry eyes.

"Why should I consider you any different from other women," he replied tersely. "It seems to me that they are all out for the main chance."

"I don't get your meaning," she snapped.

"Do not try telling me that you have no other man already lined up to step into Omar's place."

"I'm not going to tell you anything." She tossed her hair away from her face with a defiant gesture. Suddenly, the desire to shock him swept over her. "If I told you that there is someone else for me, would you arrange for me to return to London?"

She had no time to continue in the same vein before his hand shot out to grip her wrist in a vice-like hold.

"Be quiet," he growled from the back of his throat. "I have no wish to hear you say more. A residence permit has been applied for, and so all thoughts of England and the other man must be put from your thoughts."

"You might be able to tell other

women what to do or what to think about, but you can't tell me." She dragged her hand away, unconsciously massaging the place where his fingers had gripped. "Even if you have a certain say in what I do right now, my thoughts will remain my private affair." She got unsteadily to her feet, not wanting him to know how his dark surveillance disturbed her.

The door opened and Laura turned swiftly to find a slender, dark-haired girl entering the room.

"Ahmed!" The girl moved across to stand beside him. "I wondered where you'd got to. Had you forgotten that we were to ride together this morning?"

Ahmed stood up to slide a friendly arm about the girl's shoulders. "Of course I hadn't forgotten." He smiled fondly down at her before introducing the two girls to each other.

"Françoise is yet another of my cousins," he explained to Laura. "She is a nursing sister at the largest of our hospitals here in Tripoli."

"Distant cousin," the girl reminded him in her attractive voice, "once or twice removed."

"Did you train in England?" Laura asked politely, not that she was really interested.

"No. In Paris," Françoise replied. "My father is French, but my parents are divorced," she said matter-of-factly before turning to Ahmed again.

"You aren't dressed for riding." She smiled and dimpled up at him. "I do believe you had forgotten."

"Neither are you dressed correctly." He looked down at the cream silk shirt and the calf-length dark brown skirt she was wearing.

"Ah, but I am." She moved a booted leg to show off her divided skirt. "I thought this would be cooler."

"Very nice too," he replied as they moved towards the door together.

Laura sat down again, reaching out to touch the coffee pot. Not that she wanted another drink; it was just that she didn't want the other two to know

48

the true state of her feelings.

"'Bye," Laura lifted her head and forced a smile to lips that felt suddenly stiff and unyielding. "Nice to have met you."

By moving her eyes a fraction she met the cold, impersonal stare of the man who still had his arm around the girl's silken clad shoulders. "Have an enjoyable ride," she continued before turning her attention to the cold coffee she was about to pour into her cup.

3

WHAT had been her feelings as Ahmed and the French girl left the room, Laura asked herself as she drove along the road in the car her father-in-law had now told her she could use. Thinking about that moment, she recalled the way Ahmed's manner had changed towards her with the arrival of the other girl. He'd been coldly arrogant to her only seconds before, then it had been as if she no longer existed. The sneer that had twisted the well shaped mouth had slid into a smile, and the bleak look levelled at her had been charged with sudden warmth as the girl had breezed into the room. She'd never known any man to change his moods so often. His attitude towards her was confusing, and she hated him for what he was doing to her.

Laura changed gear to send the car moving at greater speed along the wide, tree-lined road. Leaving the city behind had done nothing to lessen the heat of the sun blazing down. Winding the window down she wiped the film of perspiration from her top lip, and then pushed her sunglasses higher on to her nose. Orange trees were growing in orderly rows in the groves on each side of the double carriageway, the fruit on the low branches ready for picking. At regular intervals along the roadside small boys had oranges and bananas for sale, all of them anxious to attract the eye of the passing motorist. To the left of the road Laura caught flashes of blue sea between the odd building and the sand dunes. Passing through a small village she pulled up in front of one of the shops hoping to buy something to eat and drink. The rolls on the tray smelt as if they'd just been taken from the oven. The boy behind the counter couldn't speak English but he soon understood what she wanted. Five or six minutes later Laura was on the road again, the bread and wrapped cheese stowed in the compartment beneath the dash.

If she hadn't remembered Suleiman telling her that he'd missed the turn off for Leptis on his last visit there, Laura might also have missed it. The journey had seemed less than the 123 kilometres from Tripoli, but she'd been too interested in the scenery to think about the distance. There were very few other cars parked outside the entrance gate to the ruins. Laura was pleased about this: it meant that she could stroll at her leisure, sketching anything that took her fancy. Getting out of the car, she locked the door and walked with a feeling of well being towards the gate.

Lifting her face to the warmth of the sun, Laura felt the magic of the place as she wandered from one area to another. She passed through ancient archways and stared in wonder at carvings that had been worn by centuries of wind and rain.

She brushed her fingertips over marble pillars, rested her palms flat on statues so life-like that she half expected the deep stone chests to inflate with a sudden, indrawn breath beneath her hands. Turning the corner into one of the cobblestoned clearings, she lifted sun dazzled eyes to find Ahmed leaning with indolent grace against a pillar of rose-tinted marble. She stopped walking as he started to move slowly across the space that separated them. Hastily putting her sunglasses on she opened her mouth to speak, to say hello to him, but the words wouldn't form on her lips as he stopped directly in front of her. He didn't speak either as his hand reached out to remove the dark glasses from her nose. Lifting her chin with a gentle thumb and finger, his eyes stared down at her through heavy, black-lashed lids.

"Laura," he growled deep in his throat, his arms reaching out to pull her closely against him. She knew she should have pushed him away but her heart's beating echoed in her ears, making movement impossible. He bent his head slowly until his mouth settled mothlike against hers. Feelings she'd never known before urged her to move closer to him, her hands sliding over his chest to rest about his neck. She felt his swift indrawn breath at her touch, and in that moment it was as if they breathed from each other.

"My mind is filled with thoughts of you," he said. "It has been like that since that first meeting."

His mouth took hers again after he'd kissed her eyes, her neck and the soft unpowdered texture of her cheeks. Suddenly he dragged his mouth from hers, putting her firmly from him.

"Forgive me," he said, his voice a hoarse whisper. "I had no right to do what I have just done. This place has bewitched us," he said, taking her hand. "Let us go back to the cars."

Laura stumbled with the shock of it all as they turned to walk past the pillars and the statues. His hand steadied her for a while and then she moved slightly away from him. The warmth of the sun reached out to soothe her, brushing gently across her shoulders, through her spine, until it reached her heart. By the time they reached the clearing where the cars were parked Laura's mouth had stopped its trembling, the tears dry in her eyes before they had the chance to fall.

Marvelling at her own self-control, she asked him if he'd care to share her bread and cheese. "I've also got a couple of cans of 'Coke'." She smiled up at him.

His manner was as cool as hers as they shared the food, sitting on the stumps of sawn down trees in the shady clearing. He asked her if she'd done any drawings of the ruins; Laura shook her head in reply, remembering that she had in fact left her sketch pad on one of the stone seats near the Forum. Getting to her feet she brushed the crumbs from the legs of her jeans. "More

'Coke'?" she asked, offering him the can that she'd been drinking from.

He took the can from her, putting it to his mouth to swallow the tepid liquid. His eyes met hers and she moved away towards her car, self preservation uppermost in her mind. If he touched her now, if he kissed her in the same way as he'd done earlier, she knew she would be lost. It was up to her now to show him that she wasn't someone he could kiss and caress whenever the mood should take him. She'd keep her distance from him and make certain, in turn, that he would keep away from her. He drove behind her on the way home but when they reached the garden roundabout not far from the villa she waved him on. Moving away from the roundabout she slackened speed causing him to press the horn impatiently. When she still didn't pick up speed, he passed her on the outside, his face an angry blur in the overhead street lighting. Laura could remember darkness falling, yet she must have flicked the headlights on without prior thought. When she reached the villa, Ahmed was already in the large, brightly lit room where the family congregated each evening. Before going upstairs to wash and change, she poked her head into the room to let them all know that she was back.

"Well, daughter," her father-in-law greeted her, "did you enjoy your visit to Leptis? Was it worth the journey?"

"I found it unbelievably beautiful," Laura replied.

"You should have waited until I was able to take you." Suleiman looked across at her. "It is not always safe to travel so far alone."

So Ahmed hadn't mentioned that he had also driven out to Leptis. Glancing across to the corner where he was sitting beside the elegantly dressed Françoise, Laura met his intent look with a coolness she was far from feeling.

"I was quite safe. In fact my day was

quite ordinary," she said; her reply was for Suleiman, but at the same time her eyes moved in a swift arc towards the far corner.

She looked back to her father-in-law. "I was enchanted with the city of ruins," she said. Then, greatly daring, she continued, "It is certainly a place that has the power to stir the blood. It gave to me the feeling of midsummer madness for a little while."

Let Ahmed make what he liked of that!

Laura felt pleased with herself as she left the room to run lightly up the stairway to her own room. It was easier playing that kind of game. If she could keep up this couldn't-care-less attitude with Ahmed, at least her pride wouldn't be hurt. It didn't matter that her heart still ached because of the way he'd put her from him at Leptis that afternoon.

It didn't take her long to discard her jeans and shirt in favour of a loose jade green kaftan. The evening passed as usual, the warmth of the family wrapping itself around her. Only Ahmed treated her with distant reserve, but with Françoise sitting near to him, no one seemed to notice anything different. What excuse had he made for his absence from the villa since his early morning ride, Laura wondered. The fact that he was always going off on some business or other seemed to give him licence to come and go as he pleased.

"What will you remember most about your day at Leptis?" Françoise's voice reached Laura across the width of the room.

She lifted puzzled brows. Had the other girl guessed that Ahmed had followed her there? Françoise wasn't asking out of friendly interest; of that she was quite sure.

"I dare say I shall remember everything," she answered, "but while I was standing beneath one of the statues of some dead Roman today I recalled the words of someone — Shakespeare, I think — that seemed to fit my mood."

"How did the words go?" Suleiman asked. "Poetry was always a good subject of mine, so let us all hear them. There is little need to be shy."

"I can't remember the words exactly but they were suitable for today." She hesitated for a second or two before reciting, "'I sometimes think that never grows so red the rose, as where some buried Caesar bled'."

"That might have come from Shakespeare's pen," Suleiman agreed.

"The words were written by Omar Khayyam," Ahmed said firmly, getting to his feet and pulling Françoise gently to hers.

Laura pretended not to notice when both of them left the room.

Soon afterwards she walked over to the side table to help herself to the fruit arranged in the dishes there.

"Let me get you some food, Laura," her mother-in-law said. "There is mutton, fish without scales and plenty of *cus-cus* all ready in the kitchen."

Laura assured her that she wasn't

60

hungry, merely thirsty.

She couldn't wait to go up to her room, the need to be alone seeming to be all important. At last she managed to get away, saying that the day had tired her.

Usually the nights were cold after the heat of the day, but it was so hot in her room that it was impossible to drift off to sleep. She heard the cars being driven away from the villa, and soon afterwards she heard the others retire for the night. Now everything was quiet, except for the dogs that barked out in the road.

Sliding from the bed, Laura padded across the soft carpet to stand against the window. There could be a storm brewing, she supposed, yet there was no wind, the usual forerunner of bad weather. The palm trees below in the garden were still, and the navy blue sky was full of stars, the moon floating like a huge orange balloon above the tall eucalyptus trees. Turning her head a little to the right, Laura caught the moon's reflexion on the rectangular pool adjacent to the rock garden beneath her window. The staff would be asleep in the basement apartments, and her in-laws at the front of the building. Did Françoise have her own flat? Did Ahmed spend most of his time there? Laura didn't want to think any further. A swim in the waters of the pool would help to cool her down, she decided, crossing to the chest of drawers to take out her one-piece bathing costume. She usually wore a bikini for swimming or sun-bathing, but such skimpy attire would be frowned on in an Arab household. Pulling the cobalt blue swimsuit up over her slender hips she tied back her hair, collected a towel from her bathroom, and left the villa by the side stairway. The air was cool about her legs as she crossed the path by the sunken rock garden. There was hardly a ripple on the surface of the pool before Laura dived in from the edge. The water still retained a little of the sun's heat, but the chill of it against her heated limbs made her catch her breath. Insects were still busy in the dried up grass and a night bird called out from the tall conifers flanking the grounds. Laura swam a length of the pool with slow, easy strokes before turning to float on her back to take in the beauty of the night sky. The lights of the city cast a golden glow in the distance, and the plaintive strains of music floated softly from a nearby building.

Suddenly a new sound broke the peace, a soft purring of a car's engine. Dipped headlights sketched a pale yellow path to the far side of the villa, and with bated breath Laura heard the engine die and then the gentle click of a car door being closed. Undecided whether to stay where she was or to make a dash for the stairs at the side, Laura took a deep, shuddering breath. For all she knew Ahmed might be in the habit of having a midnight swim. She couldn't risk him finding her there, and so, without further thought, she climbed from the pool and made for the corner, picking up her towel on the way. Draping the towel over her shoulders she strained her ears, trying to pick up the slightest sound. The ground floor was all in darkness now, so Ahmed had already gone up to his own quarters. She'd worried unnecessarily. Shivering with reaction, she ran lightly up the marble steps, wiping her face with the edge of the soft yellow towel. Pushing open the side door she felt her blood run cold. Her room was filled with golden light: someone was in there. With fast beating heart Laura moved into the centre of the room, wondering which course to take. At that moment the door of the adjoining sitting room opened and Ahmed Saheed filled the doorway.

"What the devil are you doing here? Get out of my room before I scream the place down." She pulled the towel closer about her.

"When I didn't find you in here, I

thought for one wild moment that you had gone," he said, running the fingers of his right hand through his thick, well groomed hair.

"I don't care what you thought. Just get out of here. What do you want, anyway?" she asked.

He looked at her for a second or two. "Would you be surprised, I wonder, if I told you," he said.

There was something in the way he looked at her that sent the wild blood leaping in her veins. She felt suddenly afraid, not of him, but of herself.

"Would you please go," she gasped. "I'm tired. I want to go to bed."

He moved closer to her. Without speaking he took the towel from about her shoulders and began to dry her dripping hair. She felt the warmth of him, smelt the spicy tang of the after-shave he used. The towel felt damp as he rubbed it across her back and shoulders, but that did nothing to put out the fire his touch had ignited.

"You are beautiful." His voice was

hoarse as his arms closed about her. "It seems the space of a lifetime since I held you this afternoon."

His hands moved down the length of her back, moulding her closer against him before his mouth closed over hers.

"No," she gasped, tearing her mouth away from his as his hand moved up to cup her breast. "Ahmed," she said, through lips that trembled, "I want you to leave. I want you to go now, this minute."

His hands fell to his sides, his eyes taking their fill of her in the damp, clinging costume. She saw the white line of tension around his mouth as he held himself in check. Seconds later he ran his fingertips along the edge of his black, polo-necked sweater, and then bent to pick up the towel from where he'd dropped it onto the carpet.

"Believe it or not," he said, "I came here tonight to beg your forgiveness for this afternoon. I had no right to follow you to Leptis."

"No. You hadn't," she replied. "I don't suppose Françoise was very pleased when you told her."

"I never discuss my private affairs with anyone," he snapped.

"Oh, come, Ahmed, no one could call our short time together this afternoon an affair. A moment of madness would describe it better," she said, moving across the room to sink onto the edge of the velvet covered chair.

"You think that?" He lifted dark brows.

Meeting his intent stare, she nodded.

"In that case, I will bid you good night," he answered quietly. "I will try not to bother you again."

With a curt nod he left her, closing the door carefully behind him.

After that little episode Laura didn't see him for a further three days; then it was just a brief greeting as they passed each other in the courtyard. She wasn't bothered, she told herself on that occasion, if she never saw Ahmed Saheed again.

When Suleiman asked her if she'd like to go to a wedding party with Jameela and himself, she agreed eagerly.

"Who's getting married?" she asked.

"A friend of mine. He's in the army. We were cadets together," he replied.

Jameela was delighted by the fact that Laura had agreed to go with them. "The wedding parties go on for days and days," she said when Laura got in beside her on the back seat of the car. Suleiman was his usual good-humoured self as they set off, telling Laura about some of the many wedding parties he had attended.

"When are you going to get married?" Her eyes met his in the driving mirror. "Or do you intend to stay a bachelor like Ahmed?"

"Oh, I shall marry when the time is ripe," he assured her, "though if the rumours are correct, I expect Ahmed will beat me to it."

She wanted to ask him what he

meant, but she couldn't frame the words. It was Jameela who urged him to tell them what he'd heard, anxious to know the name of the woman who had managed to capture Ahmed's affections.

"Françoise has hinted many times that she and Ahmed are close to each other, but everyone knows that," Suleiman began. "But I heard it mention at my place of work that an announcement was expected shortly."

Laura didn't pass comment. She'd felt from the beginning that there was something between Ahmed and the French girl. Remembering the way he'd embraced her with such passion while still having Françoise in tow, she felt a kind of shame for the way she'd reciprocated. Some men needed more than one woman: well, Ahmed Saheed wasn't going to use her to lend that extra bit of excitement to his days.

Laura was quiet after that, but the other two made up for her silence as they travelled away from the city. The road wasn't a particularly good one, having numerous potholes where the surface had melted in the heat. They left the coast road after a while and the landscape became more rugged. When they arrived at the village where the ceremony was to take place, Laura said that she hoped that their friends wouldn't mind them bringing her.

"Everyone will be happy to welcome you," Jameela assured her. "I only hope the noise of the festivities won't be too much for you."

They had to park a fair distance from the huge tent where the reception was to take place, but even from that distance they could hear the music and the hubbub of excited voices. The tent was crowded to overflowing but Suleiman shouldered a way for them, up to the place where the newly-weds were being greeted by their guests. It was as Jameela had said it would be. Both the bride and groom were pleased to welcome her. They were both beautiful people with similar limpid dark eyes and smooth, blue-black hair. Laura was a little put out by the noise at first, but returning the smiles of everyone around, she soon began to feel at ease. The air was heavy with the smell of perfume, and the dinner that was served once everyone was seated would have been enough to feed a multitude. The tent was festooned both inside and out with hundreds and hundreds of fairy lights flashing on and off as the feasting carried on. After everyone had finished eating Jameela and Suleiman introduced Laura to a great number of people, all of them eager to speak gently to the English widow of Omar Saheed; many wondering at the friendship of Laura and Jameela, the two women who had each played a part in Omar's life. But Laura didn't know them, and Jameela didn't seem to care what any of them thought.

"You did say that these wedding parties go on for four or five days and nights, didn't you?" Laura asked Suleiman. "Doesn't anyone go to bed?"

"Of course," he grinned down at her, "but only when they can no longer keep awake."

"Where are we going to stay?" she asked, adding, uncertainly, that she didn't bring anything with her.

"Both Jameela and I will be working tomorrow, so we shall be leaving shortly. Have you felt happy amongst my countrymen?" he asked.

"Yes, I have," she replied. "I'm glad you asked me to come with you." She looked around for Jameela. "Where has she disappeared to?" she asked.

"Talking to someone or other." He turned his dark head to look over the crowded tent. "It is good for her to mix. She has been restricted in the past, but now she is free to fraternize where she pleases."

"I hope she will find someone to make her really happy. She is a beautiful girl."

Suleiman looked at her for a second or two.

"When the time is right, she will find happiness again. So will you, Laura," he said, lifting his hand to attract Jameela's attention.

4

LAURA had a headache when the note was brought to her room. What was it all about, she wondered, reading the note again. Omar's father hadn't said anything to her the previous evening about needing to see her privately.

Sighing with exasperation, she reached for her hairbrush from the glass-topped dressing table. Looking closer at her reflexion in the gilt framed mirror, she couldn't help but agree with what her father-in-law had said a day or two before. She did look washed out; her eyes had definitely got a bruised look about them which no amount of sleep seemed to help. Brushing her hair with sharp, impatient strokes, she wondered what would happen if she told everyone just why she was looking finely drawn. Replacing the hairbrush, she stood up and ran her hands down her skirt, straightening it in front of the mirror before walking out of the room. Halfway down the stairs she retied the bow of the cream silk shirt she was wearing, with fingers that shook a little.

Tapping on the door of the book lined study, she pushed it open. Instead of finding Omar's father sitting at the desk, she found Ahmed waiting for her.

"Oh, it's you," she said superfluously. He looked up from the paper work on the huge mahogany desk. "Sit down, please." His long, slender hand indicated the well sprung chair. "I won't keep you a moment."

"I'll come back later," she replied, turning to walk away.

"I will not be here later." He screwed the top back onto his pen. "And what I have to talk about is important. It seems that I have been remiss in seeing to your immediate financial needs." He reached for one of the black cheroots from the box on the desk, but apparently changed his mind about taking one.

"What do you mean? What financial requirements?" she asked, sitting on the edge of the chair.

"I had forgotten that you had no ready cash." He picked up his lighter and put it down again.

"I don't need money," Laura said hurriedly. She stood up again. "Unless you are intending to lend me the money for my air fare home."

"You know my answer to that, Laura, so save your breath."

"What business is it of yours. Why should you be the one to concern yourself about my finances."

Ahmed stood up and moved slowly round the desk until he stood in front of her.

"The latter part of your question is easily answered," he told her. "Two years ago, I took over the responsibility of the family, financially and otherwise."

"I don't want you to do anything for me." She turned from him and made

76

for the door. He reached it before her.

"Hear me out, Laura, I beg of you," he pleaded, his hand coming to rest on her arm. "I have something else to say to you, something which must be said."

"Begging is definitely not your scene, Ahmed. You're one of life's winners. You'll succeed where others fail." She shook his hand from her arm.

"If I succeed, it is only because I work at it," he answered her.

Laura was suddenly lost for words. What was there about this man that left her feeling churned up inside after only a short time in his company? He had that certain way of looking at her that made her foolish heart rejoice at his nearness. But it shouldn't be like that. Soon he was to marry Françoise, and before that happened, she would have to be thousands of miles away.

"May I go now, please?" she asked breathlessly. "I need to go to my room."

Without another word he reached for the door handle. Turning it, he stood back so that she could go from the room.

Half an hour later, as Laura was looking through the window of her room, she saw Ahmed's Range Rover being driven along the back road.

In an effort to relieve the boredom of the long afternoons, Laura began to spend more time with Omar's mother and the two aunts. She found it pleasant to sit in the shade given by the dusty palms, listening to the chattering of the women. Not that she was able to understand much of what the aunts had to say. Her mother-in-law translated most of the conversation and in this way Laura was able to get a closer insight into the life of the Arab women. The old aunts belonged to a more restricted way of life than the women of the present day, and listening to the remarks made by her mother-in-law, Laura realized that even today, Arab women weren't as liberated as the ones from the Western world. She began to look forward to these afternoon get-togethers, finding them restful, to say the least. She saw little of Ahmed, but just knowing that he was around from time to time was enough. This attraction she felt for him would go in time, she told herself whenever thoughts of him disturbed her sleep. There were times when she knew without being told that Ahmed had gone off on one of his business trips. Sometimes it was just for a couple of days, others a little longer, but at these times there was a coldness about the place that had nothing to do with the temperature. Laura couldn't define the feeling, but when he returned her nerves would tingle with a new awareness. Where did he go to and what did he go away for, she wondered, surprised in a way that this wasn't discussed during the evenings. After all, it was usual for all matters concerning the family and their friends to be discussed at this particular time.

On the evenings when Françoise put in an appearance, Laura would glance up to find the French girl watching her. She felt the girl's animosity, and wondered if perhaps Françoise was annoyed by the new closeness that now existed between her and Mrs Saheed. On one of the occasions when Françoise arrived early, she confronted Laura, accusing her of showing too much interest in Ahmed.

"You've no reason for concern," Laura told her. "I know you and he are to be married shortly. I don't make a habit of seducing other girls' men."

"Yet you took Omar from Jameela," Françoise sneered.

"You've got a spiteful tongue," Laura gasped,

"I'll show you how spiteful I can really get if you don't leave my man alone. I find the way you hang on to his every word quite sickening."

"I hardly see Ahmed these days."

As if she hadn't heard the last remark, Françoise continued, "He finds your flirtatious manner annoying. He assures me that he has tried to talk to you about the way you try to monopolize him, and also about your free and easy manner with Suleiman. Each time he tries to speak to you on the subject, however, you make some excuse to get away."

Laura met the spiteful gaze levelled at her. Françoise's words had startled her, but in no way was she going to let her know it. Instead she smiled in a cool, collected manner.

"You should learn not to be so possessive," she said. "I'm sure Ahmed is man enough to tell me what he considers I should know."

With a confidence she was far from feeling, Laura made her way out of the villa to stand for a while in the darkened quadrangle where her father-in-law grew exotic plants. Lifting her hands against cheeks that burned, humiliation washed over her as she recalled the other girl's angry words. In that moment she knew that it wasn't what Françoise had said was responsible for the feeling; it was knowing that Ahmed had discussed her with

Françoise. Remembering those times when he'd insisted that he must speak to her, she felt a bigger fool than ever. Why the devil hadn't he come straight out with it. What had she done or said that could have shown the way she felt about him. She had always schooled herself not to appear to be too pleased to see him, nor had she looked his way more than courtesy demanded. It was only in the silent darkness of her room that she ever allowed her thoughts the delight of running riot. She'd tried to snap the thread of attraction that spanned between them. He had been the one to try to force the issue, so what gave him the right to discuss her in that derogatory way.

A soft wind sighed through the cracks in the walls of the secluded area. The moonlight filtered through the unshuttered windows, throwing the shapes of the exotic plants in sharp relief. Knowing that she couldn't stand there all night, Laura made her way back into the villa. Someone was playing a guitar, and the sound of laughter filtered into the entrance hall from the larger of the ground floor rooms. With the silk of her dress brushing softly against her ankles, and her head held that fraction higher, Laura reached for the ornate door handle. It was in that split second before the door actually opened that she remembered that Ahmed wasn't expected back until the following morning. Relief washed over her. It would have been just too much to feel the magnetism of his presence and to know at the same time that she was nothing but a source of irritation to him. Forcing a smile to play about her mouth she pushed open the door of the beautifully furnished room. Greeting the family in turn, as was the custom in the Saheed household, Laura met the amused blue eyes of the tall bearded man standing beside Suleiman.

"Meet Steve," Suleiman greeted Laura. "He's a compatriot of yours."

She found her small hand engulfed

by the much larger one of the good looking man.

"Hello," she smiled. "I thought for one moment that you were another of the cousins."

Steve explained that he was a field operations manager with the oil industry. He had known the Saheeds for almost five years and often spent his leave from the desert at the villa. When Laura explained her reason for being there, he told her that he already knew about her.

"I'm sorry about young Omar." He looked down at her from his superior height. "It must have been very distressing for you."

"It was hard on his parents. They had such hopes for his future."

Why was it that whenever someone mentioned Omar, the feelings of guilt were pushed up from the depths of where she tried to hide them. Noting the haunted expression that flashed across her face, Steve's hand touched her elbow.

"You won't get over it by hiding away from things," he told her. "You should get out, see the different aspects of the country. There's plenty to see here."

"Suleiman has taken me around the old and the newer parts of Tripoli, and I've also visited Leptis Magna."

"You should see it all. The desert, too, if you have the chance. That place has an enchantment all of its own. It has moods like a woman and is just about as changeable."

"You sound as if you could be an expert on both counts," she laughed.

"You can say that again," he assured her, the smile slipping from the well shaped mouth.

Laura was glad of Steve's company over the next few days. His easy going manner was infectious, giving to her a confidence that she'd found lacking in herself since arriving in the country. His presence gave her something to lean on, a prop that enabled her to greet Ahmed, whenever they met, with a casual smile. She knew by the brooding look on the dark, hawklike face that Ahmed read something more into this friendship of hers with the tall, bearded oil man. She was glad because of this. At least it would prove that she had no designs on him. Françoise seemed pleased about it all, even though she couldn't resist telling Laura that Steve had been very fond at one time of the English girls working at the clinic.

"What happened to your romance with the nurse?' she asked Steve when he was bringing her home from a party one night.

"That's something I'd rather not talk about if you don't mind," he replied, covering her hand as it rested on her knee.

"Is it still painful?" she asked, watching the road unfurl in front of them, in the glow cast by the headlights as he drove along the almost deserted carriageway.

"Mm, a bit." He gave her a lopsided

grin without taking his eyes from the road. "She will come to her senses in time, to realize just what she's missing," he replied, in that conceited manner that Laura found very appealing.

"You aren't as brash as you like to make out," she said. "I know your bigheadedness is just a veneer to hide a gentle sensitivity."

"It seems that you know me almost as well as I know you. Who is the man in your life, mm?" he asked, shattering her mood of complacency.

"Has there got to be a man in my life?" she asked carefully. "I could still be longing for the might-have-been."

"Your eyes have a bruised look, yet whenever we are away from the villa you manage to laugh, and thoroughly enjoy yourself," he reminded her. "And, what is more, you haven't got the look of a woman pining for what might have been. I don't say that you don't miss young Omar, we all do. It just seems to me that another man could be responsible for the lost look about you."

"I shall just leave you wondering about me." She turned in her seat.

"I hope Suleiman isn't the one," Steve continued quietly.

"Why," she asked, "because he's Omar's cousin, you mean?"

"That fact wouldn't matter to a family as caring as the Saheeds," he replied. "They would consider it quite correct for you to be cared for by one of Omar's kinsman. It's just that I know that Suleiman has his eye on Jameela."

"If Jameela shares his feelings, then I'm glad for both of them."

"I do believe you mean it." Steve braked to take a corner.

"Oh, I do. I'm very fond of both of them," she assured him. "I'd rather you didn't probe too deeply into what you think you know about my romantic longings. It could lead to more heart-searching than I feel up to, right now."

Steve told her that he had only been making a wild guess. "If there isn't anyone now, there will be, some day. Things have a habit of levelling off. In the meantime I'll be on hand to keep you amused."

Over the next couple of days Steve was true to his word. Laura enjoyed being with him. She found his extrovert manner refreshing, to say the least. He took her to Misurata, to see how the beautiful, local carpets were made from the wool of the country's sheep. Laura was fascinated by the roadside scenery, and Steve never tired of taking her to places way off the beaten track. They explored caves honeycombed within the hillsides, and tiny dwellings built below ground level.

Laura was really excited about their visit to Sabratha, another of the country's historic ruins.

"The Phoenicians chose this place as one of their trading posts because of its natural harbour," Steve explained. "It seems different to me every time I come here."

He enjoyed showing her over the

museum, pointing out the oil lamps and the coins that had been found there over the years. When they left the museum to walk into the heat of the deserted, ancient city, Steve put her quietness down to the atmosphere of the place. They walked through the theatre and the amphitheatre, with the sun beating down on the golden brown rocks. The sea below that was a calm, clear blue, almost the same colour as the beautifully preserved mosaic flooring. South-west of the Byzantine walls stood the Mausoleum of Bes, the bow-legged dwarf once highly honoured by the Phoenicians.

"The Phoenicians used to set images of Bes on the prows of their ships to ward off evil." Steve took hold of Laura's hand. "Bes is by tradition the conqueror of lions and the protector of the dead."

Laura wondered why her interest in the ruins had suddenly evaporated, but when Steve stopped walking to stand in the shade cast by a stately marble pillar she knew the reason for her change of mood. Her eyes had taken in the beauty of Sabratha, but her heart had been longing for that other ruined place and the man who had followed her there.

"What is it?" Steve lifted her chin. "Have I tired you out?"

Laura shook her head, afraid to lift it in case he should notice the tears that threatened to fall. The sun glinted on the thick gold chain Steve wore about his neck, then his arms closed about her, pulling her to rest against him. He kissed her then, a gentle caress that took a little of the hurt away. She found it pleasant being kissed by him, but he wasn't Ahmed, and so her need of him finished there.

On the way back to Tripoli they stopped for a meal at a small roadside restaurant.

"There's nothing like food for reviving the flagging spirit." Steve grinned at her across the table, his fingers smoothing his well-groomed dark beard.

"Do you shampoo your beard?" she

asked as she felt the tension relax.

"Sometimes." He took hold of her hand and squeezed it. "Feeling better now?"

Laura nodded. "Thanks for being so patient with me, Steve. I'll do the same for you some day."

"Just being with you has taken a little of the sting out of my days. In fact, I shall miss you when I go back to the desert."

She asked him about his work and about his way of life before he came out to Libya. He answered her questions in an interesting way. He told her that he'd been married but was divorced a few years later. He told her about the days of his youth and about his mother's house in Norfolk, but not once did he mention the girl François had told her about.

They didn't speak much once they were on the road again but by mutual consent they stopped at a small quarry village, parking the car while they visited Christian catacombs and the tomb of one, Aelia Arisuth. It was as they walked back to the place where they'd left the car that both of them became aware of the new, unnatural warmth of the late afternoon. Perspiration trickled down the back of Laura's neck and prickled in a film across her top lip. Everything seemed unnaturally quiet, even the birds had stopped their singing.

"What is it, Steve?" she asked. "Is there a storm brewing?"

"It's the start of a *ghibli*, the hot, dry wind that comes up from the desert. It usually carries clouds of sand with it," he explained. "We'd better get a move on while visibility is still clear."

Steve was a competent driver, and Laura felt no fear as he drove with speed in an effort to beat the arrival of the hot, sand-filled wind.

"Do you have strong winds out in the desert?" she asked in an effort to show him that she wasn't worried.

"Sometimes the sand dunes are as high as a block of flats," he told her, his eyes screwed in concentration. "A strong wind can blow one side of a dune away until it looks as if it has been sliced by a giant knife.

"Does rain follow the wind?" she asked, wondering how long it would take them to get back to the villa.

"Sometimes a hail storm precedes the rain, but after it is all over the dust settles and new life springs up in the *wadis* and the dried up river beds."

Laura watched the sky darken as the clouds moved in from the sea. The force of the wind made strange noises as it lashed the palm trees, bending them almost double along the side of the road. Sand lifted in dusty swirls, making visibility almost nil. It was with a distinct feeling of relief when Laura spotted familiar landmarks. With luck they would be home within the next ten minutes. She noticed that all the shops were now shuttered, and that the windows in the blocks of ultra modern flats were covered by slatted blinds. Of course, they were the *ghibli* blinds that

Mrs Saheed had mentioned when Laura had asked her about the wooden slatted blinds that could be dropped over all the windows of the villa. Thunder rolled overhead, and Steve told her that this wouldn't stop until the rain began to fall.

"There's one thing, petal," he said laughing, "our day at Sabratha has certainly ended in a blaze of heat and noise, if not in glory."

"Are storms always as fierce?" she asked.

"Sometimes the *ghibli* blows for days, but it seems this one is going to be short but none the less ferocious."

They found the approach road to the villa covered in sand.

"Seems they've got the windows well barricaded against the storm. Sand gets in everywhere," he said, turning the car into the side drive. The trees and bushes growing in the garden swayed in time to the whining of the wind, their branches robbed of their blossoms that had been a riot of reds and yellows only hours before.

"We'd better make for the back door. The wind isn't quite as strong there," Steve said, as he pulled the car up by a sheltered wall. He got from the driver's seat and raced round to let her out.

Hot sand stung their cheeks and arms as they mounted the steps to the door.

"Hope they can hear us above the sound of the wind," Steve said, lifting his hand to the bell.

Before he had the chance of pressing the bell, the door was dragged open from within. Looking up in swift amazement, Laura saw Ahmed standing there, his face a mask of savage ferocity. His eyes had a feverish glitter about them, their gaze unwavering as he looked down at her, ignoring the man at her side.

"I have been out of my mind with worry for you," he said at last.

"Come on, Ahmed, let us in, man." Steve broke the moment of tension. "We're getting blown about out here."

"Of course, forgive me," Ahmed replied, stepping to one side so that they could enter the wide marbled-tiled hall.

Passing by Ahmed, Laura felt him looking intently down at her. She turned her head, but didn't look any higher than the dark column of his throat above the open-necked shirt he was wearing.

He touched her shoulder. "The force of the storm does not distress you?" he asked, his voice sounding strange, quite different from his usual assured way of speaking.

Laura drew a shuddering breath. "No, I'm all right," she said. "I'm ready for a long, cooling drink, though."

Throughout the evening that followed Laura felt Ahmed's eyes on her, and knew that Steve was also aware of the intensity of that stare.

"You're playing with dynamite there," Steve whispered to her at one time. "Ahmed isn't a young, inexperienced boy. A hawk like him could destroy a dove like you."

"You forget that he is to marry Françoise," Laura reminded him.

"That's just gossip," he told her. "Françoise shares only a small portion of Ahmed's time. He's a polished man of the world, and well used to the adoration of women."

All the same, Laura was glad that the French girl wasn't present that evening.

After the meal had been cleared away, the men became involved in a complicated card game. Catching her mother-in-law's eye, as she looked up from her embroidery, gave Laura the opportunity she had been waiting for.

"Would you mind if I went up to my room?" she asked. "I guess the day out and the storm have made me tired."

"You should have gone earlier," the older woman replied in her usual gentle manner. "I shall also retire." She folded the brightly coloured silks and wrapped the linen panel she was working on. "Sleep well, daughter. We will meet in the morning. *Insh' Allah.*"

Laura said good night to the others and then left the room. The wind had dropped a short while ago and torrential rain lashed against the shuttered windows. She had intended taking a shower but ran a bath instead. It was pleasant relaxing in the hot, perfumed water, feeling the tight knots of tension slipping away. What would she have done without Steve, she wondered, reaching forward to turn the hot tap on again; and how would she get through the days once he returned to his work in the desert. There was only one course open to her. She would have to make it clear to Omar's parents that she had a right to return to her own country, and to pick up her old way of life there. Steve had told her that once she left Libya behind her she would forget Ahmed and the attraction she felt for him. But she didn't want to forget him, she told herself as she reached for the soft yellow towel and stepped out of the bath. She didn't ever want the pain of loving him to fade. Once she was back in England, she would be able to think about Ahmed without being afraid of letting anyone else know the true state of her feelings. At least she'd be able to look back to this time and know that she'd been able to leave with her pride intact. After all, pride was the only thing left for her. A precious commodity in anyone's book, even though she knew it would be a cold and lonely bedfellow.

5

"**I**T seems to me that you are spending too much time with my guest," Ahmed greeted Laura one morning just after the storm.

"Am I responsible to you for my every action?" Laura asked, reaching for the coffee pot from the middle of the breakfast table.

She felt him looking at her and glancing up swiftly she surprised a look of brooding malevolence.

"I suppose the next thing you will want to find fault with is the way I dress," she snapped, looking down at her blue and white striped tee-shirt and narrow legged jeans.

"I don't care a damn what you choose to wear, Laura. It is the late hours you keep, and the time you spend alone with Steve that give me cause for concern," he said.

"I shall go where I like," she replied.

"In fact, if I decided to go into the desert with Steve, that wouldn't be your business either," was her cool reply.

"Into the desert?" He lifted puzzled brows. "That would be frowned upon, I can assure you. I only hope nothing of the sort has been arranged between the two of you."

When she didn't answer he suggested that if she really wanted to take a short trip into the desert it would be safer if a number of people made the trip together. "I would be happy to join you, and perhaps Suleiman would also add his name to the list," he said. "Not only would it be incorrect for you to go alone with Steve, it would also be unsafe."

"I'll talk it over with Steve when he comes to pick me up later," she replied, before getting on with her breakfast.

Laura marvelled at the new, crisp way they had of talking to each other; but of course he didn't know just how much his nearness affected her.

When she did eventually mention to

102

Steve about the possibility of a desert trip, he thought it was a good idea.

"You could find it very tiring, though," he said, "even though part of the journey could be made by air."

Almost before she knew it, the trip had been arranged, but instead of Suleiman being amongst the proposed travellers, Ahmed had asked Françoise to join them.

"How long are we going for?" she asked Steve.

"Only for a few days," he grinned, the sunlight slanting across his lean, good-looking face. "It will soon be time for me to report back to work, and it seems that Françoise has only managed to get a week's leave from the clinic."

"Couldn't you have arranged for that other girl, the one you used to go around with, to come with us?" Laura asked impulsively.

"Gloria is on leave right now. Gone to Rome with some friends of hers. It wouldn't have done any good even if she hadn't been away," he said. "It's over; everything that was between us is dead, finished. I thought you understood that." He reached over to run the flat of his hand down the length of her hair, his large hand settling on her shoulder.

At that moment Ahmed came into the room, and for some inexplicable reason Laura felt the hot colour sweep up to her cheeks. About to pull away from the hand that had by now slipped to her shoulder, she felt the sudden pressure of Steve's fingers. It was almost as if he urged her to be still as Ahmed came up to them.

"Françoise will be over shortly to tell you what you will need," the low pitched voice coldly informed Laura.

"Oh, that's OK. Steve has already instructed me. He bought me one or two necessary things yesterday, as a matter of fact."

Ahmed turned his head to look at Steve.

"How much did you spend?" he asked him. "Let me know and I will reimburse you."

Laura found herself staring at the harsh lines of the hawk-like profile for a second or two before Steve said that he didn't expect to be paid for the things he'd bought for her.

"That may be permissible in your country, but while Laura is here, that duty is mine," Ahmed replied in no uncertain terms.

"Tell you what, Ahmed, you buy Françoise some things and I'll buy whatever Laura needs." Steve moved his thumb in a circular motion on Laura's shoulder.

The two men, both the same height, stood face to face.

"If Laura wishes it to be that way, then there is nothing else to say." Ahmed turned to walk across the room. "By the way," he added, "if you get every-thing packed today, Haj Baloo will take it down to the old airport in readiness for tomorrow's early morning flight."

Steve watched him walk away, a puzzled frown wrinkling his brow.

"Ahmed has always been an arrogant devil, but just lately it seems that our friendship of the last five years is about to fizzle out," he said thoughtfully.

"I find him overbearing at times," Laura replied, moving away from Steve.

"But there are times when you find his presence necessary." He laughed softly.

"Does it show?" She turned to face him.

"Only to me, sweet, but don't let that bother you. Your guilty secret is quite safe with me."

He told her that once she'd seen Ahmed in, what some would consider to be, his own environment, she might not feel the same attraction for him.

Laura knew that that wouldn't be so. It wouldn't matter to her where he came from or what he did. What she felt for Ahmed would always be the same, but she didn't bother telling Steve that.

When Françoise joined them later in the day her former, brittle manner towards Laura was replaced by a new friendliness. Her dark eyes sparkled with mischief whenever Steve said something amusing to her, and when Ahmed came into the room she made no secret of the way she felt about him. Looking at the two of them as they stood side by side, Laura wondered how long it would be before the news of their forthcoming marriage was made public. It seemed that the family had not yet been informed. When Laura had mentioned it to her mother-in-law earlier that morning, the gentle, doe-like eyes had turned to her, a puzzled expression in their depths. Realizing that she'd spoken out of turn, Laura had hastily changed the subject, speaking instead about the trip to the desert.

Their luggage was taken to the city's older airport by the white-robed Haj Baloo, and immediately after the evening meal Ahmed suggested that the two girls should have an early night.

"You will have to be up before the

dawn." He gave Laura the benefit of one of his rare smiles. "You must be fresh and wide awake by then."

Good nights were said, and Laura walked up the wide stairway with Françoise, who was also staying the night in readiness for the early morning departure.

"You've been to the desert many times, I suppose," Laura said.

"Of course," the other girl said, and grinned appealingly. "You forget that I'm only half French, the other part of me is Arab."

"Do you like the desert?" Laura asked.

"In small doses." Françoise smiled, showing her small, perfect teeth. "But it isn't so much the location as the company one is with. Just to be with Ahmed, without the family always being present, will make the trip perfect. There will, of course, be the other relatives there but they are different, not so correct if you get my meaning."

"Oh. I didn't realize that we were to visit relatives."

"You will be entertained by them all, I can assure you. The festivities that take place whenever Ahmed returns are unbelievable. They treat him like you British treat your Royalty."

They parted at the top of the wide landing, Laura going towards the back of the villa, Françoise to the east wing.

Laura didn't think sleep would come easily as she slid between the cool sheets, but the alarm of the bedside clock was just about to ring when she opened her eyes again. Stretching luxuriously, she flicked on the light and then slid from the bed to pad over to the bathroom. She had showered and was already dressed in the loose cotton *jellaba* Steve had advised her to wear, when one of the servants brought coffee and hot rolls to her room.

The morning air was cool as Haj Balloo drove them out to the old airport where they were to get the special desert plane; Steve, looking like some bronzed sun god in his light weight khaki suit, walked beside Laura as they passed the sheds and huts before crossing the tarmac to where the F-27 waited for them.

"Though this crate lacks the sophisticated comfort of the usual passenger aircraft, you'll find the views more interesting," Steve told Laura as he took the seat beside her.

She smiled briefly in return before shifting her position to look out of the window of the cabin. Tripoli still slumbered, the traffic quiet, except for the odd truck that lumbered along the perimeter road. Glancing upwards, Laura noticed the pink wash of dawn edging the clouds as the plane took to the air. Looking down, she watched the land mass dropping away beneath them, the buildings and roads of the city stretching out in orderly precision. The plane banked, moving southward, away from the blue waters of the ocean and heading out towards the open desert. The further they travelled away from the coast, so the *wadis* lost their greenery. Palm clumps became less apparent, and settlements further apart. It seemed only a short while later when Laura stared down over a landscape of gleaming white sand stretching out endlessly beneath them.

"It has a forbidding look about it, this desert of yours." She turned to face Steve.

"You'll find it a fantastic place," he assured her. "That's if you stand the dust and the heat."

"What is it about the desert that gets you?" She rested her fingers on his bronzed forearm.

His hand closed over hers. "I came out here at a bad time in my life," he replied quietly. "The years of hard work, the difficulties one comes up against, all helped me to find a certain peace. Now that particular bad time seems a million years ago."

He told her then about the marriage that had floundered, and about the divorce that followed.

"It seems that romance and I aren't good partners," he said smiling self-consciously for him.

"You'll find the right one some time, Steve. You've got to if the law of averages is to be believed." She returned the pressure of his fingers. "What about the nurse from the clinic? What went wrong there?"

"I guess I was just plain scared of getting hurt. Gloria must have found my lack of serious intent upsetting, breaking off our relationship before I had the chance of proving to her just how much she really meant to me."

"People don't change all that quickly, Steve. She'll come to her senses."

"But people do change, Laura. I know that from first hand experience."

"Don't be a defeatist, Steve. It doesn't suit you." She lifted his hand, cradling it against her cheek in a gentle, caring gesture.

Glancing across the aisle separating the double row of seats, she felt the icy flick of anger from the dark hooded gaze levelled across at her. Ahmed had discarded his tailored suit in favour of his Arab robes, but the face beneath the white headdress was none the less dear to her.

"Fasten your seat belt, honey. We're about to land," Steve informed her.

She felt the plane begin to lose height, but suddenly, because of Ahmed's obvious dislike of her, the prospect of spending even a short time in the desert had lost much of its appeal. The heat haze shimmered across the landing strip, and as soon as the doors of the aircraft were opened the heat rushed in to meet them. Leaving the plane, Laura looked about her, feeling her senses quicken with reborn interest.

"At least the wind is quiet," Françoise said, moving to stand beside her while they waited for their luggage to be taken from the plane.

Uniformed men, machine guns at the ready, stood guard at intervals across the width of the small airport. Camels rested in the shade given by a clump of palm trees, and a herd of goats shifted small hooves in the hot, dry sand. There was little of the hurry and bustle attached to larger airports, but security was none the less stringent.

"The remainder of our journey will be made overland," Ahmed said as he came up to where the two girls waited. "Our baggage has just been stowed aboard the Range Rover."

It was hot inside the vehicle but the air felt cooler once they were on the move. Steve was in the driving seat, Ahmed beside him, the two girls seated behind them.

"Do you usually drive a Range Rover in the desert?" Laura spoke to Steve's broad back.

"No. I use my own Chevvy truck," he said, taking the road away from the airport. He told her then about the huge treadless tyres that he used on the special wheels of his pick-up for travelling across the sand.

"Are we going anywhere near to the plant where you work?" she asked.

"You wouldn't find it at all interesting there, honey, though I'm sure all the men would enjoy seeing you around." Steve laughed.

"If you did take her out to the plant, you would finish up with a riot on your hands. Perhaps it would be better not to put ideas into her head." Ahmed's tone was frosty.

For the rest of the journey Laura gave her attention to whatever she saw from the windows of the Range Rover. Heat bounced from the tall dunes of pale sand. Small bushes and scrub grew at infrequent intervals, and, thinking of the consequences of being lost in the forbidding Libyan desert, Laura had difficulty in suppressing a shudder.

"You aren't cold, surely." Françoise looked at her with concern.

Laura shook her head. "I was just thinking how easily one could get lost out there," she said.

"That is why great attention is given to taking extra water bottles and extra petrol on journeys of any length,"

Ahmed said, without turning his head.

"Anyone travelling to the plant or from it has to leave details of all journeys and the routes to be taken. That way it is easier to track anyone who doesn't report on time," Steve added.

"How do you know which way to go? Everywhere looks the same."

"By using the compass, honey," Steve replied matter-of-factly.

They passed a larger cluster of palm trees, and the dark smudge on the horizon proved to be an oasis of considerable size.

Men wearing colourful robes to protect them from the fierce rays of the sun appeared in the clearing as the Range Rover drew to a halt in a cloud of dust. Children arrived as if by magic, all of them eager to greet Ahmed and his companions.

Ahmed, his face losing a little of its former fierceness, got out of the vehicle and then turned to open the door for Françoise to alight.

"All right, pigeon?" he asked her before moving round to open the other door for Laura. Immediately her feet touched the sand, he turned abruptly to walk away from her. She in turn took a shuddering breath of the warm desert air, and smelt the unmistakable aroma of meat being roasted on the spit. Looking about her she noticed the tents pitched beneath the palms, and the two pitched near the far end of the clearing.

"Those are for us." Steve spoke from behind her. "One for Ahmed and me, the other for you two ladies."

"I hardly thought one would be for you and me," she answered saucily.

"That may be the way in your country," Ahmed said, coming up from behind her.

"I dare say the same thing happens here from time to time," she replied meaningly. "People are human the world over."

Now why had she started the conversation in the first place, she wondered. By the time she'd finished he'd consider her morals to be lower than low. Not that it mattered either way, she decided, walking silently across the sand, feeling the gritty warmth of it as it seeped through the open weave of her sandals to cling between her toes.

As they reached the two separated tents, Ahmed opened up the wide front of one of them. "I hope you will find the accommodation comfortable," he said. There were two sections to the tent, one for each of the girls. Soft, hand-woven rugs covered the sand floor and colourful blankets were draped across each of the narrow beds.

"Someone will bring you water in which to wash, and sherbert to drink," he told them. "Then I would advise you to rest awhile; unless, of course, you feel the need for food."

Both of them refused the offer of food. "How will we know when it is time to get up?" Laura asked.

"Get up when you are rested," Ahmed told her before he lowered the outer flap of the camel skin tent.

Françoise told Laura that she would rest for a while and then she would visit the tents of her various cousins.

Laura wondered if she would survive the heat as she splashed over her face the cool water brought to the tent. It was a relief to kick off her sandals and to stretch out on the comfortable bed.

The air was decidedly cooler when Laura eventually got up from the low camp bed. It was dark in the tent but she caught the flickering of lights filtering through the partially open flap.

"Françoise," she called, "are you awake?"

Getting no reply she crossed the softness of the hand-woven rugs and lifted the dividing curtains. A battery fed storm lantern stood in the far corner, casting shadows across the empty bed. Reaching for the lantern, Laura carried it into her own section of the tent to flick open her small suitcase. She decided that the full length peasant style skirt and soft brown mohair jumper would be ideal for the evening ahead. She was just brushing her hair when Steve called her name from outside the tent.

"Coming," she answered, putting the brush down on top of her case.

She was quite unprepared for the colourful scene that met her eyes as she stepped out into the clearing. Torches flared at intervals between the tents and a huge fire blazed in the centre of the clearing. Stars twinkled in the navy blue sky, and with the moonlight and the flaring torches the whole effect was bright as any day. Dishes of food were set out on a huge table standing barely six inches from the ground, with the robed men, women and children sitting on the ground around it. At the far end, facing the circle, an open fronted tent had been pitched, the heavy fringing around the front flirting in the evening breeze. It was to this tent that Steve escorted Laura.

"Ahmed's uncle, he's the chief of this little lot, is waiting to meet you," he said, as they walked past the laughing, chattering people.

Laura felt her heart skip in her breast when Ahmed moved from the shadows towards them. The firelight gave his face a ruddy glow, and for one brief moment it was as if he stared into the secret garden of her heart. Without speaking to her, his fingers settled gently around her elbow. Steve stepped back, and she walked towards the tent beside the tall, cloaked figure. Françoise was already seated to one side of the white robed figure, who stood up as Ahmed and Laura stopped in front of him. She met the highly intelligent stare and felt the warmth of the older man, who stood up to welcome her. She would have known without being told that he was Ahmed's kinsman. The heavy, black lashed lids were the same, though the creases around them were deeper.

"Welcome to the oasis," the deep voice greeted her. "I hope you will feel at home amongst my people." He sat down, making room for Laura to sit beside him.

An assortment of food was brought towards them and after the customary "in the name of God", the eating began. Barbecued chicken and lamb, herb flavoured beef, curried rice, spiced semolina, all to be eaten with the fingers. Ahmed's Uncle Mohammed was an avid conversationalist, discussing many things with Laura between the different courses. They discussed the early cultures of both Britain and Libya, and then passed on to talk of the present day.

After the remains of the meal were cleared away, they watched an exciting display of Arabic dancing. From time to time, Laura looked up to find Steve's amused blue eyes upon her, and she wondered if he realized that she was acutely conscious of Ahmed standing immediately behind her. She felt the warmth of him, felt the roughness of his cloak against her cheek whenever she moved her head. Later, as the torches burned lower in their sconces, she felt his strong fingers settle on her shoulder, to pull her gently backwards until she rested against him. The fingers moved from her shoulder to brush across her nape as the musicians in the clearing changed their rhythm, and the haunting tones of a female singer dropped like honey on the smoky air. When Ahmed's fingers touched the cheek furthest away from the others, Laura turned her head slowly to rest her lips with a swift, moth-like pressure against his fingers. She felt him tremble against her, and when in that same moment his uncle turned his head to speak to her, she had great difficulty in forming a reply.

"Yes," she managed at last, "I have enjoyed every second of tonight's entertainment. It was all quite unexpected."

The spell was broken and the entertainers were about to leave the clearing. Françoise, obviously not wanting to be left out, joined in the conversation. When the old man got to his feet, she also stood up, moving behind the three seats to stand beside Ahmed.

"All right, honey?" Steve moved towards Laura.

"Fine," she smiled, trying to hear what Françoise was saying to Ahmed.

"The sun has caught your nose." Steve laughed down at her, running his fingertips across the bridge of her nose. "You'll have to put cream on it or you might start peeling."

She made some amusing reply, blushing with confusion when she turned to find Ahmed watching her across the width of the tent. The look was an uncaring one, almost as if he was bored by it all. Of course. Laura bit her bottom lip. He had been bored by the evening's entertainment; he'd seen it all before. The interlude during which he'd touched her furtively had been nothing more to him than a pleasurable diversion. She was suddenly annoyed with herself for reciprocating.

The proud old Arab chose that moment to say good night, and it seemed only natural that Laura and Steve should walk with him towards his larger, more ornate tent.

When Steve asked her if she wanted to look at the moon for a while, she laughingly refused. "I feel in need of my beauty sleep," she told him, anxious now to get to her own tent before Françoise returned.

But she needn't have bothered to hurry. She was in bed and almost asleep before she heard the other girl drop the outer flap of the tent.

Laura slept fitfully throughout the night. She listened to the strange music of the wind as it sighed through the branches of the nearby palms and the noise of the camels snorting to each other in the darkness.

The following morning there was no sign of Ahmed. She wondered if he had decided to leave the area for a day or two, but couldn't bring herself to ask about him. Towards mid-day, the old

125

uncle sought Laura out, asking her to share a mid-morning glass of *chai* with him. She had intended telling him that she didn't much care for the green Libyan tea, but thought it a small price to pay for the pleasure of listening to him. Later, when he introduced her to another of his kinsmen as Mrs Saheed, Laura lifted puzzled brows; but when the other man mentioned Omar, she remembered self-consciously that Saheed was indeed her legal name.

Mentioning the fact that she hadn't seen Steve all morning, old Mohammed told her that he was helping with the horses for the afternoon's display of Libyan horsemanship. Françoise came out just then to join them, telling them without embarrassment that she'd only just got up.

"Time has no meaning out here in the desert." She smiled beguilingly from one to the other, and not for the first time Laura wished that she could hate the other girl.

As the time for the display drew near

the air was charged with a new excitement. Men wearing their colour-ful robes stood a little apart from their *baracan*-clothed womenfolk. The two girls accompanied the old man to the open fronted tent again, taking the same seats as they had the night before. Laura heard the chinking of the harness only seconds before the group of veiled horsemen rode at speed across the clearing. She'd read somewhere about the fierce horsemen of the desert tribes, and watched the display with a breathlessness quite new to her. At the end of the performance, when the men dismounted and removed the veils that had kept the dust from their faces, she saw, with pleasurable surprise, that Ahmed had been the lead rider of the group.

The longing to run to him, to feel his arms about her, swept over her. It didn't matter that his moods could change swifter than the wind. She wanted him, needed him, the longing to hold him becoming a physical pain.

With something of a shock, Laura realized that she had actually taken a couple of steps towards him. What could she be thinking about? Ahmed neither needed her nor wanted her. Françoise, the one who was now racing across towards him, was the woman in his life. She, Laura, had no right to think otherwise.

6

"WELL, honey, what did you think of your short stay amongst the desert tribe? Did it come up to your romantic expectations?" Steve took her hand as their aircraft took to the air.

"I loved the people. In fact, the last few days have been quite educational," she answered, over brightly.

"You'll get over it." He squeezed her fingers, glancing swiftly to the opposite seats where Françoise was listening avidly to whatever Ahmed was talking about.

"When do you return to the plant, Steve?" Laura moved her position to look at him as she spoke.

"In a couple of days," he told her. "Just as soon as the equipment I'm waiting for arrives. Why?"

Laura was thoughtful for a while.

"Because I don't want to be in Tripoli after you go away."

"For one wild moment I thought my luck had turned." He gave her a lopsided grin.

"Be serious, Steve." She tapped his hand. "We're just friends, and you wouldn't have it any other way. You don't need to pretend with me. I know where your heart truly lies."

"What you really want is for me to smooth the way for your departure. Am I right?"

"Mm. Something like that. Ahmed still has my passport, and you know how he is about family ties. He thinks he is now responsible for my welfare."

"Leave it to me, sweet; but once the step is taken, there can be no stepping back for you. Only you and I will know that what I have in mind has no significance. All you'll have to do is to just play along."

There was no denying the dismay of Omar's mother and father when, during the course of that evening, Steve mentioned that he intended taking Laura home to London the following day.

"But Laura's home is here with us," Mrs Saheed reminded him.

"It was until today," Steve explained carefully. "Now that Laura has agreed to marry me, she is my responsibility."

Listening to him, Laura had difficulty in keeping silent. It didn't seem fair to deceive the Saheeds in this way. She might have explained to them, told them, that this was just an amusing joke on Steve's part, if Françoise, who had entered the room in time to hear Steve's announcement, hadn't congratulated Laura on beating her into matrimony.

"Ahmed. You'll never guess." The French girl turned as Ahmed's tall figure entered the room. "Laura and Steve are to be married. Isn't it all exciting?"

Laura didn't know how she managed to get through the next few hours. She felt like a hypocrite, accepting the good wishes from the family and friends who came to the villa later that evening.

"Big Steve will take good care of you," Jameela told her. "But why go back to London? If you stay here you will be on hand whenever he takes his leave from the desert."

"I must go back. I don't wish to stay here any longer," Laura replied, smiling to take the harshness from her words.

Finding herself alone with Steve, she asked him if there had been the need to be quite so drastic in pretending that an engagement existed between them.

"That's the only way you could be certain of being able to leave. You are Omar's widow, remember, and the Saheed family have looked upon you as their responsibility. Now they are content to give you into my keeping."

"But you won't have the time to take me to London."

"I'm going to Malta in the morning to see what can be holding up the consignment of equipment I've been expecting. You will come with me there, then later in the day I'll put you on board a flight for Heathrow. It's as simple as that."

"But what about later, when they find out that we didn't get married after all?" she whispered.

"I shall tell them that you changed your mind," he said, grinning. "After all, isn't that supposed to be a woman's privilege?"

Marvelling at the cool efficiency of the man, Laura found herself playing the part of his future wife with light-hearted pleasure. It was only when she said good night to her mother and father-in-law, before they retired for the night, that she felt the ache of sadness for needing to deceive those caring, loving people.

Ahmed had been strangely silent for most of the evening, but when Laura said good night to him, her foot on the bottom step of the stairway, he asked her to spare him a moment of her time.

"Come into the study," he said. "I

133

have something to give you. Something that rightly belongs to you."

Laura looked anxiously round for Steve, but he was outside in the lighted driveway looking at Suleiman's new car.

"I won't keep you any longer than is necessary," Ahmed told her, leading the way across the Turkey red carpet towards the study.

No sooner were they inside the book-lined room, the lights on and the door closed, when Ahmed turned to face her.

"Why, Laura? Just tell me why," he said.

"I . . . I don't get your meaning." She played for time.

"This speedy arrangement to marry friend Steve," he continued, a harshness touching his well defined mouth. "I find it hard to believe that this new attachment of yours has been allowed to flourish with few of us noticing it. I didn't believe, until Françoise pointed out the familiarity that existed between you and the man I considered to be my friend."

Laura returned his burning scrutiny. "What has Steve's friendship with you to do with it?" she asked. "What I wish to do with my life has nothing to do with you."

He looked at her in such a way that if she hadn't known better she would have thought his dark-lashed eyes pleaded with her.

"It seems that I've been mistaken, then." He pulled his tie free from the collar of his white silk shirt. "This . . . closeness I thought existed between us from time to time was something I imagined. Is that what you are telling me?"

"You came into my life when I was lonely and upset. I'll admit that there have been times when I've been grateful for your attention. But we both knew that there was no depth, no lasting element between us; so let's leave it at that, shall we?"

He listened to her and then slowly

looked her up and down in that infuriating way of his. For once Laura was glad because of this. She couldn't afford to weaken now. Better to make the clean break than to be tossed aside when he'd either had enough of her or married the other girl.

"You are very cool, Laura, I'll say that for you." He turned to cross over to the wall safe. "I have given your passport and your exit visa to your future husband," he informed her. "Now I will give you part of the dowry that your late husband planned for you to have."

"I don't understand," Laura gasped. "I know nothing about a dowry. I've told you that before."

"Most of my countrymen give gold to the woman as part of the marriage contract. Omar put yours into this safe the day before the accident. I know he would have expected me to give it to you in his absence."

He removed the leather covered boxes from the safe as he spoke, placing them on top of the inlaid mahogany desk.

"Go on. Open them," he ordered.

"I'd rather not, thank you." She stepped back, intending to walk from the room.

He moved towards her, grabbing her wrist with a savage ferocity. "I said, open them, then you can tell me if my cousin paid highly enough for the pleasures you undoubtedly gave to him."

With nerveless fingers Laura lifted the lid of the first box. A triple roped necklace of gold rested on the narrow bed of red velvet. She touched the necklace gently and then lowered the lid.

"If that isn't to your liking, try the next one," he ordered her.

When she didn't move he lifted the lid and took out the wide chain link belt with the distinctive clasp of twin camels. The light caught the bright gleam of the gold belt as it swung from his fingers.

"This should look well about your slender waist," he said, dropping it with a clatter onto the polished top of the desk.

"I don't want to see anything else, Ahmed," she said as he reached out to flick open the lid of yet another of the narrow boxes. "Let them stay in the safe."

The fight had gone out of her, she felt saddened and defeated.

"What, and let Omar's parents consider that their son's gift to you were not important? You could always sell them. Gold like this will fetch a good price on the open market."

"I have no right to Omar's gifts," she said, ignoring his gibe.

"You have no need to pretend with me, Laura. I am quite certain that you gave my young cousin much better value than the gold."

"I gave him nothing, damn you. Nothing at all. We were never lovers. There wasn't the time."

Before he could stop her she dashed

138

from the room, not caring who witnessed her wild flight.

It was Suleiman who offered to take Laura and Steve to the airport just after lunch the following day. Of Ahmed there was no sign; only Mr Saheed was there to wish Laura a safe journey. He explained that his wife wished to be excused, saying that the thought of saying goodbye would be too painful for her.

While Steve and Suleiman stacked the luggage into the boot, Laura thanked her father-in-law for the kindness that had been given to her during her stay at the villa.

"Your home is here should you ever feel the need," the voice so like Ahmed's told her.

"I'll keep in touch," Laura replied, "and we'll meet again, some day."

"If God is willing." He bent to kiss her on both cheeks before she turned to walk down the steps to where the car waited for her.

After going through the usual

formalities at the airport, Laura waited impatiently for their flight to be called. For the first time she didn't know what to talk to Steve about. Once they were on board the plane, however, then tension eased between them.

"Did you notice that no one asked us when we were to be married?" she remarked to Steve as the plane began to taxi across the runway.

"Ahmed did," he replied.

"What did you tell him?" she asked.

"Told him to mind his own damned business," he said, an amused little smile playing about the mobile mouth above the well trimmed black beard.

Turning to look through the window, Laura watched the patchwork of fields and road dropping away. Seconds later she watched the clear blue waves rolling up the shore, then in what seemed to be no time at all the plane began its descent into the early afternoon heat of Malta.

"Once we've checked your baggage

in, we'll go up to the restaurant," Steve said, noting the weary droop of Laura's shoulders.

Later, as they sat at one of the tables drinking coffee, he gave her his post box address in Tripoli and also the address of his mother's house in Norfolk.

"Keep in touch, girl," he said, taking hold of her hand as it rested on the table.

"Of course." Her reply was over-bright. "And don't you forget to call on me whenever you get the chance. Tell you what," she continued, "I'll cook you a superb meal, the very next time you are in the UK. After all, that's the least I can do in return for all you've done for me."

Steve looked intently across at her. "I only hope we've done the right thing," he said slowly. "Seeing all that pain in your eyes, baby, makes me wonder if it might have been better to leave things as they were."

"I'll be OK once I get back into my

own little niche again." She laughed, but the sound was cracked, off key.

"It wouldn't have worked out with you and Ahmed, though." He tried to reassure her, running the edge of his thumb across the back of her hand. "He's too autocratic. Omar was different. He was softer, more like his mother."

Laura's flight was called seconds later. "Come on, girl." Steve pulled her gently to her feet. "Let's get the show on the road."

"When will you be going back to Tripoli?" she asked, as they walked towards the departure gate.

"Tomorrow, perhaps, but I shall go straight out to the plant. I don't suppose I shall see your in-laws for a while, unless of course Ahmed visits the plant, as he often does."

Stopping at the end of the passenger queue, Steve slid his arm about her shoulders.

"Well, baby, be good." He smiled down at her. "And don't forget about keeping in touch."

His lips were warm as they brushed across hers, and then picking up his pigskin grip he turned and walked away from her.

She watched him go, lifting her hand to return his wave before his tall figure disappeared through the entrance of the airport.

Laura tried to sleep during the flight from Malta to Heathrow but she had to make do with just closing her eyes. The first thing she noticed on landing was the cold, biting wind. It had been winter in Libya also when she'd left there, but she'd found it quite hot compared with what England offered weatherwise.

"Could be snow blowing up," one of the other passengers remarked, seeing her shiver at the thought of having to face an English winter again. Once she'd collected her luggage from the baggage carousel, Laura telephoned through to her landlady to let her know that she was on her way.

The first few days in familiar surroundings passed by with relative ease. On the Tuesday morning, Laura applied for the job of artist with a travelling theatre company. It wasn't the sort of thing she really wanted, but the members of the company seemed a friendly lot. When the director saw the folio of sketches and paintings that she'd taken with her to the interview, he asked her if she would do an impromptu sketch suitable for the backcloth of one of the theatre's current productions. Well pleased with her effort, he offered her the job.

Day followed day in a multi-coloured world of stage scenery, props and amusing companionsip. It was only in the silence of the night that Laura allowed herself the luxury of thinking about the might-have-beens. Whenever she closed her eyes in the quiet darkness of her room, the strong features of Ahmed Saheed flashed across the screen of her lowered lids. Her landlady remarked about the weight Laura appeared to have lost, but, looking at her figure in the full-length mirror, all Laura noticed was that her waist was perhaps a little smaller and to her critical eyes only made her bust look bigger.

At the end of the month the theatre company moved up to the Midlands to fill engagements at several small theatres in the area. Afterwards they moved on to Britstol and the West Country. Spring came and went away, and it was about the time when the May blossom frothed across the hedgerows that Jim, the astute Scots director of the company, bought an old barge moored on the canal bank in a quiet backwater, a mile or two from the busy market town.

"Is it for business or pleasure?" Laura asked when he told her about his purchase.

"Oh, business," he replied, telling her about his plans for fitting out the barge as a floating theatre. "Not this year, of course," he assured her, "but I would like you to see what you can do with the paintwork."

About to remind him that she was not a painter and decorator, he told her about the carvings of hearts and roses around the barge. "The paintwork on the carving has all flaked off. It will give it a fresh brightness if you could spend a little time on it," he said.

It was agreed that Laura should stay on the barge to touch up the paintwork once the repairs to the timber had been completed. By that time the company had been booked for three separate weeks in neighbouring towns near Cheltenham. When Laura was first left on her own on the gently moving barge, she imagined that she would miss the stimulating company of the others. She was surprised, however, to find that this was not the case. The work was absorbing, the peace of the warm sunny days delightful. She'd never been quite so near to nature before. She began to recognize the different flowers growing along the bank. Each day she watched the swallows swooping low over the water, taking their fill of the small flies and insects, before zooming upwards again. Bees droned on the warm air, going back to their hives as the cooler evening approached. Each day the barge had a brighter look about it. Once the main part had been given a complete new coating of black paint, Laura began the more intricate painting of the scarlet and green flowers and leaves, and the cobalt blue and yellow hearts. Sleep came easier after the day's work, and Laura grew quite fond of her makeshift bed in the small cabin. Listening to the creaking timbers and watching the moon scudding between the clouds through the small expanse of window were the last things she remembered until the early morning light teased across her eyelids. She collected eggs and milk daily, from the farm a short distance along the tow-path, walking to the village for the rest of her shopping. When rain came towards the end of the second week she had to leave the painting, spending her days reading in the cabin, and listening to her transistor radio. Once the rain had been blown away, the day dawning bright and clear, Laura was glad to get on with the work again. She heard the tractors busy on the farm, and saw the cows and sheep in the nearby fields. Few people walked along the towpath, but those who did stopped awhile to admire her work, and to pass the time of day.

When she saw the postman riding towards the short cut to the farmhouse, she stopped working, her paint brush held half way between the paint tin and the bunch of realistic looking oak leaves she had just been touching up. With some surprise Laura watched the post-man leave his bicycle against the fence, walking towards her with letters in his hand.

"For you. m'dear, if you are Mrs L Saheed." When Laura nodded, he handed over the envelopes forwarded on to her by her landlady. Watching the postman riding away again before sitting down on the warm timbers to tear the envelopes open with swift, eager fingers, she found that one was from Suleiman, telling her that he and Jameela were to be married after the feast of Ramadan. Laura felt happy at the news, but knew she would have to turn down the invitation to the wedding when it arrived. The second letter was from Steve. He expected to be in the UK shortly, he had written, in his large, untidy hand, and was hoping to see Laura during that time. He explained to the Saheed family that they were no longer engaged to be married. "Though I did tell Ahmed that we intended to review the possibilities at a later date."

Laura read and re-read that portion of Steve's letter before refolding it and putting it back into the envelope. Though neither Suleiman or Steve had mentioned anything about Ahmed's engagement to Françoise, a little of the joy seemed to have gone from the day. For the remainder of the afternoon Laura's brush moved more slowly across the beautifully carved leaves and flowers. The creative pleasure had disappeared, and shortly afterwards Laura cleaned her brushes and fastened the lids back on to the tins. In an effort to keep thoughts of Ahmed at bay she jumped from the barge to the bank. The overhanging tree cast its long shadow across her; the sunlight filtering through the branches dappled her face and tanned bare arms as she stood there.

Damsel flies were at work on the surface of the water, floating across in a silvery mist, moving faster than the eye could see. The afternoon was heavy with birdsong, the dark water of the canal contrasting with the jewel brightness of dragonfly and bee.

Laura had secretly hoped that Ahmed would have written to her. That was one of the reasons she had asked her landlady to post on any mail that arrived at the house for her. She was certain of one thing now. The emotional feelings she had cherished for the man who seemed equally at home in the desert or in the city had not been reciprocated. Ahmed had merely enjoyed playing with her. Holding her face up towards the sun, Laura closed her eyes against the glare. She felt the warmth on her cheek and knew a yearning for the fiercer heat of the desert. Angry with herself for allowing the longing for Ahmed to cloud her day, she jumped back on board, deciding to get on with the painting again. There was only a little more work to do now. Once it was all finished, she could leave the quiet haven on the waterside and get back to living once again. Remembering brought only heartache. Work was the thing she should lose herself in.

When Jim came to collect her at the weekend, he was delighted with the way she'd transformed the appearance of the old barge. He told her on the journey to Stratford that he had made arrangements for the barge to be taken to new moorings not far from his own home.

"Next year it will be one of the floating theatres that seem to be quite popular these days," he said. "Meanwhile, we'd better concentrate on the bookings we have in hand."

7

THE summer days were warm, the roses in full bloom, when Steve arrived back in London. Laura found him waiting for her at the house after she'd spent a busy day touching up the scenery ready for the company's next booking.

"You look good enough to eat, paint streaks and all," Steve greeted her.

"You look tired," she told him, looking at him critically. "You should have made yourself a drink, got something to eat," she said, plugging in the electric kettle.

He said in reply that he had half expected having to wait on the doorstep for her return. "But after I told your landlady that my name was Steve and that I was on leave from Tripoli, she unlocked the door with her pass key. I haven't been here much more than half an hour," he told her.

"What do you do besides this painting work of yours? Any boy friends on the horizon?" he asked her, as they drank coffee and ate the sandwiches she'd made.

"Some." She answered the second of his questions first. "But no one of importance. As for pastimes, I read now and again and I've completed my first portrait, a small one of Omar. Perhaps you'd like to take it to his mother when you go back to Tripoli."

"It's a very good likeness," he said as she lifted the covering from the small canvas. "Don't you want to keep it for yourself?"

"I'm pleased with it, but I'd like Omar's mother to have it," she said.

When she suggested cooking a meal for them later, he insisted that they should go out to a typical French bistro on Queensway. "The food is good there. Besides, the place holds special memories for me," he said, getting to his feet. "Be ready by eight, mm?" He smiled, leaving a couple of minutes later to go to the nearby hotel where he'd booked in earlier.

Later, as she dressed, slipping her arms into the black and gold kaftan she'd bought during her stay in Tripoli, she wondered about the man who had actually paid for the kaftan for her. Did Ahmed ever think about her? Did he care what became of her? More important, was he married to the French girl yet?

She was ready and waiting by the time Steve called for her.

"You've lost weight, honey," he said, but his eyes appraised her just the same.

"So have you," she countered, noting for the first time the few silver threads amongst his thick, dark hair. "How much longer are you intending to work out in the desert?" she asked, as they walked out of the house together.

"Until the end of my contract. Only a couple more years, then I may come back home to settle down."

He opened the door of his hired car for her, and then moved swiftly round to take his seat behind the wheel. He fastened his seat belt and advised her to do the same before setting the car in motion.

"Do you find it strange driving on the left hand side of the road again?" she asked.

"Not really," he said grinning, without taking his eyes from the road in front.

It didn't take them long to get to the bistro, but it took Steve rather a long time to find a parking area within walking distance. "I sometimes think it's quicker to go by Underground," he said, as they walked along the pavement to the restaurant he had in mind. The door was open, the smell of French cooking greeting them as they stepped inside the quaint, low-ceilinged room. Laura looked about her with interest as they were escorted to a table at the far end of the already crowded little restaurant.

The food was delicious, the red wine of Château Lafitte being the perfect fillip to the meat course. Laura hadn't intended ordering a dessert but one look at the trolley proved her undoing. The sweet, fruity flavour of the white wine from Perigord that Steve chose to accompany the almond based concoction topped with thick whipped cream, was the ideal choice.

"I didn't think you knew so much about wine," Laura said after he'd explained to her a little about the wines of Burgundy, Alsace and the subdivisions of Bordeaux.

"Even though drink isn't to be bought in Libya, I've got a pretty good memory of the wine I've drunk in my time. In my student days I worked during my vacations in the vineyards, and consequently most French wines are close to my heart."

"You are a romantic." Laura smiled at him across the table. "Tell me," she said, "have you seen anything of your Gloria lately?"

"I saw her once, just after you left. It seems our friend Françoise broke her neck to tell Gloria about our so-called engagement. Now all chances of a reconciliation are over. She gave me this back," he said, taking a ring from the inside pocket of his jacket.

Laura stared down at the exquisite half hoop of diamonds and emeralds.

"I didn't know you'd given her a ring. You've never mentioned it before," she said.

"I gave it to her eighteen months ago, just before the big row I told you about. Although I've often said it was all over between us, there was always the hope in the back of my mind that she might come to her senses. Still, that's how it goes."

"Oh, Steve, what can I say? If you hadn't been so keen to help me, everything might have been all right by now. Would you like me to write to explain to this girl of yours?"

Steve shook his dark head. "No. If she can't accept my word, if she can't learn to trust me, then the future holds no hope for us."

"Give her another chance to listen to you," Laura advised. "Go to see her, take her out, talk to her, that's the least you can do."

"You're very good at giving advice, honey, but you don't take it, do you?"

"What do you mean?" she asked.

Steve met her anxious eyes. "You are still pining for Ahmed Saheed. You can't deceive me, love."

Laura was thoughtful for a moment before replying.

"I don't waste my time pining for him. What would be the use? But yes, I still think about him. I've tried to get interested in other men, but they've nothing to offer me; nothing to fill the void knowing him has left in my life."

She asked him then if Ahmed was well and happy.

"Oh, he's well enough but one can never tell whether he's happy or not. You know what these strong, silent men are like."

"What did he say when you explained about our 'broken' engagement?" she asked.

"He didn't have the chance of saying anything. I told him that it might only be a temporary break. He seemed to think we'd had some sort of argument, a lovers' tiff, if you like, but the rest of the family make up for his lack of friendliness towards me. Ahmed Saheed is the least of my troubles."

He mentioned then that he had heard that the nurse he'd been engaged to was due to return to the UK.

"Her contract will soon be completed," he said. "Once she moves back here, I don't stand a chance of patching things up with her."

"Why don't you go back there, then? Spend the rest of your leave in Tripoli. Sweep her off her feet, marry the girl," she said. "After all, you don't have to spend all your leave here in London, do you?"

During the coffee stage Laura knew

that Steve was considering what she had just said. But it wasn't until they were walking along the street to pick up the car that he mentioned that it was a good idea of hers.

"Tomorrow I will drive down to Norfolk to say hello to my mother, and give her the presents I've bought her from Libya. The following day I will do the shopping, get the things I need to take back to the desert. Then I'll fly back to Tripoli the day after that."

He slid his arm about her shoulders. "You really are a honey," he said. "I'll send you a telex if everything turns out well between Gloria and me."

"And where do you intend to send the telex to?" she asked mischievously.

"Oh. To the consulting agency that handles the things for the company. They'll let you know the news, I expect, but I'll have a word with their very efficient secretary before I go back."

The following day Steve went off to Norfolk, leaving Laura a list of some of the things he'd promised to take back to his colleagues in the desert. They'd agreed to shop for the other things he needed, the day after he returned from visiting his mother.

It was while they were both doing the round of shops that Laura saw the exquisite chess set in an antique shop window.

"Would you have room to take that back with you?" she asked. "I'd like to send a gift to Omar's father."

"Something as beautiful as that will certainly cost you," he said. "Have a good look round before you decide. But I'll take anything back for you, you know that."

Laura couldn't find anything quite so delightful as the chess set.

"It's right, if you know what I mean. I can imagine Mr Saheed playing with it."

"No doubt friend Ahmed will be a worthy opponent," he reminded her as they waited for the shop assistant to wrap the set. Laura had already imagined Ahmed lifting the beautifully carved chessmen with his long, slender fingers. Perhaps he'd spare a thought for the girl who had sent the gift to his uncle.

Before Steve left for the airport, he asked Laura if she intended going out to Tripoli for the wedding of Suleiman and Jameela.

"No, I shan't be going," she replied.

"The Saheeds will expect it of you, Laura. You are, after all, very close to them. The old man asks for news of you every time I see him."

"Suleiman said that they expected to marry shortly after the feast month of Ramadan," she said. "I don't really know exactly what the Ramadan is. Oh, I know it's a time of fasting, but that's all I do know."

"Ramadan falls on the ninth month of the Islamic year. During that month Muslims throughout the world must abstain from food, smoking, drink and sex through the hours between dawn and sunset. It's hard, I bet, especially in the heat of summer."

"What about sick people? Surely they don't have to obey the fasting rule?"

"No. There are certain dispensations."

"When do the others eat and drink, then?" Laura asked.

"The fast is broken after sunset, then the people devote themselves to the things that are forbidden during daylight hours. This goes on for the whole month of Ramadan."

"How do they know when the month is officially over?"

"As soon as the new moon is seen, the guns boom out across the land. Several days before that, the housewives begin to cook the different food and cakes ready for the feast of *Eid El-Fitr*, the feast that marks the end of the holy month of fasting."

Laura's eyes were alight with interest. "Tell me more," she said, shifting her position so that she could look across at him. They were having coffee in her room prior to his leaving, but the coffee in Laura's cup had been left to go cold, ignored because of her interest in what he'd been telling her.

Steve smiled indulgently. "On the morning of the feast," he continued, "the men, wearing their Arab robes, go to the Mosque while the women prepare breakfast. Children are given presents and a good time is had by all."

Glancing at the complicated-looking watch strapped to his broad wrist, he stood up.

"I'd better be on my way," he said.

Laura, who had taken a couple of days leave from work, suggested that she should accompany him out to the airport. "It's no trouble to get the tube back from there," she said. "Besides, it will give us a little more time to talk."

The roads were congested with mid-morning traffic as they drove out towards Heathrow, but they managed to keep up a steady flow of conversation in spite of this.

Laura mentioned the fact that before going to Libya, she hadn't known that it was an Arab Republic.

"Libya has had a very chequered life,

as no doubt you have been told. I believe that some time during the first part of the eleventh century, two powerful Arab tribes came to Libya. They integrated with the natives, bringing with them their Islamic culture; though I have read works by a couple of historians who say that the Berbers, or Libyans, are descendants of earlier Arabs who lived first in old Yemen, then later in Palestine."

"Omar told me that his father's people were Tuaregs from the southern part of Libya."

"Yes, that's correct. Remember the kinsmen of the oasis? They inhabit the southern desert."

Laura went with Steve to take the hired car back, travelling back to the airport with him in the car company's courtesy transport.

She waited with him until the number of his flight was flashed onto the television screen.

"I hope things go well for you, with your nurse, Steve," she said, "and thanks for coming to see me. You've brought . . . everyone a little closer."

"You can't get him out of your mind, can you?" He gave her a lopsided smile. "If things had worked out differently for you and Ahmed, I still think you would have felt out of your depth. Their way isn't ours."

"Every barrier can be broken between intelligent, caring people," she told him, "and I cared enough for the two of us."

"Keep praying then, little one," he said, kissing her with fond affection. "I'll see you at the nuptials of Suleiman and his bride."

"I wouldn't bank on that," she said. "I'll keep in touch, though."

He watched her walk away, a slender, dark-haired girl who caused many a masculine head to turn as she crossed the length of the foyer.

When Laura went back to work the following day, she agreed to help the wardrobe mistress to repair the various costumes.

"I can sew a fine seam with the rest of you," she told the other girls who were also helping out. "But don't think you're going to get out of painting with me at a later date."

The job she was doing wasn't anything like the one she'd expected to do during her time at the art college. She found it quite enjoyable, though, and wouldn't change it now for a stuffy studio in any advertising agency. Her artistic know-how didn't have much chance of flourishing, except on the scenery and backcloths she designed and executed. She seemed to spend most of her time just touching up the paintwork and generally making herself useful. It was great fun. There was no chance of ever feeling lonely; all the members of the company were a friendly lot.

During the latter part of the summer their engagements were to be mostly overseas.

"That sounds interesting." Laura looked up from the costume she was mending when one of the others mentioned this. "How long do we stay away?"

"We usually get back here just before Christmas; then the rehearsals for the new productions start all over again," Lesley told her.

It was rumoured that the first overseas engagement of the season was to be in Denmark, others said Hamburg, but it was something of a shock to Laura when the notices went up on to the board. The first country they were to visit was Malta. Once there, she would be within one hour's flying time from Tripoli.

8

LAURA received the invitation to Suleiman's wedding on a morning when she was feeling particularly vulnerable. She read the accompanying letter with an eagerness that surprised her. The family worried about her, Suleiman had written, and all of them were looking forward to her homecoming. She must always think of the villa as home, because, after all, she belonged there now, didn't she?

Laura re-read the last sentence again. Wasn't home supposed to be where the heart wanted it to be. If that was so, then the villa was her home. She had the longing to see Ahmed, to hear the gravel depths of his voice. It didn't matter to her in that instant that he was committed elsewhere. Her longing was almost a tangible thing. It was almost as if her heart ached for love of him. Even though she knew that his future was tied up with Françoise, she knew that she attracted Ahmed, even though it might only be in the most basic manner.

Giving her memory full reign, she relived that magical time amongst the ruins of Leptis Magna, and the unforgettable moments when his fingers had caressed her cheek, unbeknown to the others, as they watched the display of dancing and singing while they were at the oasis. She closed her eyes, remembering the warmth of him, reliving the feelings, the excitement she'd known in his presence. That night, after a day when he'd been in her thoughts for most of the time, Laura dreamt that Ahmed's arms held her close. She wakened briefly about dawn to find that it was only a dream, the figment of her longing. When she opened her eyes later, she found her cheeks damp, the salt of tears on her mouth.

No. She wouldn't go to the wedding. To see him with the French girl might be her undoing. It was best that things stayed as they were. No doubt he had already forgotten her and the magical moments they had shared. Nothing could be gained from any further meeting between them. She would be the only one to suffer, and so the wedding of Suleiman and Jameela would have to be out of bounds as far as she was concerned. She'd buy a suitable wedding present for them once she arrived in Malta. It would be easier to ship it over to Tripoli from there, she decided, closing her mind to the memories of Ahmed Saheed.

To celebrate the last of the season's performances in London, Jim had arranged the usual party for the members of the theatre company. The studio looked a different place with the long tables set out down the length of the large room. A portable bar had been fixed on the low stage, the curtains fastened back, the gaily painted screen that Laura had done hastily at Jim's request, stretched out behind the bottles and the glasses.

For most of the evening Laura found herself being hemmed in by two of the newest members of the company. Robert and Peter were both amusing to be with, but after a while the quieter Robert moved off with Judy, leaving Laura with Peter. His good humour was infectious, and by the end of the evening Laura felt happier than she had done for weeks. The arrangements for the flight to Malta were arranged without a hitch, and almost before she knew it, Laura was at the airport once again. The plane took off on time and sitting beside Judy on one side and Celia on the other, Laura looked forward to a comfortable flight.

When the duty-free trolley came along the aisle, pushed by one of the attentive members of the cabin crew, Laura decided to purchase a bottle of her favourite perfume. She was unlucky, however. The perfume she always used was out of stock. Perhaps she would be lucky on the return journey, the air hostess told her, after trying to sell her something else in its place.

Malta was only a short distance away as Laura reached down to return her purse to the red leather flight bag at her feet. Seat belts were fastened and the aircraft began to lose height. The sea was a deep, cobalt blue beneath them, the buildings white in the heat of mid-afternoon. The three girls were almost the last to leave the aircraft, just managing to squeeze on to the last bus waiting to take them to the terminal building. It was after they'd been through passport control and through customs that Laura realized that she hadn't got her purse.

Catching up with the rest of the group, she explained her predicament to Jim.

"Hang on, everybody," he said to the others, "I'll just see what can be done about Laura's purse." He turned to

Laura as they walked back to the information desk together. "Was there any identification in the purse, an address or anything?" he asked.

"Yes. The address of my bedsitter, also my Banker's Card and, of course, my money, about a hundred pounds sterling."

"Traveller's cheques?"

"No." Laura shook her head. "They are with my cheque book in the front pocket of my flight bag."

While they waited at the desk for one of the uniformed men to attend to them, Jim glanced impatiently over his shoulder to where the others waited with their luggage.

"You go to the hotel, Jim. Once I've got things sorted out here, I'll take a taxi; I'm quite capable, you know."

"If you're sure." He touched her gently on the shoulder. "Perhaps I'd better get the others up to the hotel. Ring me there if there's any bother."

Laura watched him hurry away and then turned to speak to the dark-haired man who came to stand at the other side of the desk. He was very understanding, asking her to sit down somewhere while he arranged for someone to go out to the aircraft. "Where were you sitting, madam?" he asked. "What was your seat number?"

Before he went away, Laura gave him the stub of her boarding card with her seat number written on it. People were milling about, the air filled with the noisy excitement attributed to most airports. Suddenly it was as if the noise was switched off. Lost in the sensation of faintness stealing over her, Laura wondered if the man wearing the dark suit moving purposefully towards her could be the figment of her imagination, the culmination of too much longing.

But there was nothing unreal about the hand that gripped her arm, the dark eyes meeting hers.

"I thought my eyes deceived me." Ahmed spoke first. "Are you in transit, on your way to Tripoli?" he asked.

"No." Laura shook her head. "The theatre company for whom I work is to be here in Malta for the next two weeks. Then we go on to Rome."

"This company of which you speak, why are you not with them? Why are you alone in this place?"

She told him then about her purse, afterwards asking him what he was doing in Malta.

"I am on my way to London," he replied. "It was my intention to visit you there. I have letters for you from the family."

"I'll take them now, if you like," she said, as he manoeuvred her away from the desk to stand away from the people waiting for the next flight to arrive.

"My luggage is by now on board," he told her. "I will bring the letters back with me when I return next week. You will perhaps dine with me here in Malta."

"Post the letters to my hotel here from London," she said. "That will be the simplest thing to do."

"I will deliver the letters personally," he replied in his arrogant, no-nonsense way. "We will also need to discuss the plans for your presence at the wedding of Suleiman and Jameela."

She told him that she wouldn't be able to get away. "I work for my living," she reminded him.

"No excuse is needed." He looked down that hawklike nose of his. "Your presence will be required. So inform the person in charge of this theatre company you are at present involved with."

"I said, I won't be going," she insisted.

"We will discuss all that when I return in seven days. Keep that evening free for me."

"But you may decide not to break your journey here. If you do go direct to Tripoli, will you post my letters on to me?"

"I will return via Malta, of that you can be certain. By the way, Laura, it will not be wise of you to try to hide your whereabouts from me," he said. "I shall know where to find you."

She was saved from making a reply by the return of the airport official. He explained that the cleaners had been on board the aircraft but no one had seen the missing purse. The aircraft had subsequently taken off on the continuation of its journey, but a telex had been sent requesting a further search at the next port of call.

"And so you are without money?" Ahmed said, after the man had moved away.

"No. I have traveller's cheques," she told him.

"But you have no Maltese currency to pay for your taxi to your hotel," he reminded her.

She assured him that Jim, the director of the company, would settle with the taxi driver once she got to the hotel.

But he would have none of it. "Come. I will see you into a cab and I will pay for your journey in advance. I would take you to your hotel but it is important that I get this next flight."

About to refuse his offer of help, she met the narrowed gaze levelled down at her and consequently changed her mind.

As he turned to help her into the waiting taxi, he held her hand against his cheek for a moment. "Think of me, Abibi, until we meet again," he said, his deep voice just above a whisper. Then, lifting her fingers to his mouth for a brief second, he stood back, closing the door behind her.

She met the amused eyes of the taxi driver as he too turned to watch Ahmed walk back into the airport building before setting the cab in motion.

"Very generous, these Arab gentlemen." He turned to give her a wink as they were held up at the corner. "But then, they can afford to be."

"The gentleman is a member of my husband's family," she told him and wondered afterwards why she'd bothered.

Jim and the others were sympathetic about the purse, but they all assured her that it would turn up eventually.

Laura hadn't told any of the company much about her private life. They knew she had been married and widowed within a short time. They also knew her married name was Saheed but that she preferred to be known by her maiden name. It wasn't until they were half way through the first week that Laura asked for the following Saturday off. She knew there would be no difficulty. It wasn't as if she was one of the actors who were needed for all performances.

Everything seemed to be going very smoothly with the performances, and when she remarked to Jim that she hadn't expected the company's production to go down so well abroad, he told her that so many people spoke and understood English and that the theatre's productions were always well attended.

"We usually play to full houses like

this," he said proudly. "In fact, we're often better patronized than we are at home."

Ahmed hadn't arranged any particular time for their meeting. He had mentioned dinner, however, and so Laura imagined that he would call to the hotel for her about seven o'clock. With the whole day free in front of her, she decided to walk to a stretch of beach that always seemed to be deserted in the early morning. At least she would be alone, free to think without interruptions.

The wind was quite strong, whipping her hair about her face as she walked across the sand. Sea birds called overhead and far out on the horizon a ship sailed on to some distant part.

Looking back towards the town where the buildings followed the road along the hill, Laura was reminded of some mediaeval picture in a history book. At that moment a plane circled overhead, its undercarriage down as it came in to land at the nearby airport.

Annoyed at this intrusion, Laura turned to walk on again, her face held into the teeth of the wind. She walked at a steady pace, thinking all the while. Meeting Ahmed again even for such a brief time, had thrown her completely off balance. She had imagined that she'd been able to build up a good resistance against the attraction Ahmed Saheed had for her. Now she knew that all her resistance had been blown away like a puff-ball in the wind. She loved him just as much as she'd always done.

Turning to the left, after climbing across an outsize boulder beneath an overhang of rock, she came face to face with the man who filled her mind.

"Ahmed," she breathed, his name a glad cry on her lips. "I . . . I didn't expect to see you until this evening."

"I spotted you from the window of my room at the hotel," he said. "I got in late last night," he explained.

He looked different, more carefree with his dark hair windblown, the collar of his blue denim shirt lifting about his chin.

She couldn't remember afterwards if it had been she who had moved towards him or whether he'd moved to her. All she knew was that his arms were about her and that their hearts kept time with each other.

"You smell of the wind and the sea," he said, bending his head until his mouth met hers.

There was none of the old restraint between them throughout the day. They had breakfast together at one of the roadside cafés, and afterwards they went on a sightseeing tour of the island in a bright-wheeled, horse-drawn carriage. Later, when Laura suggested that they should go to their separate hotels for a rest in the heat of the afternoon, Ahmed pulled her close against him. "I can't be parted from you, so don't suggest anything like that again," he said, his dark eyes devouring her.

"But what about the letters you have for me? I'm anxious to read all of them," she replied, placing her finger tip across the narrow cleft in his chin.

"I will give them to you while we dine this evening," he said. "In the meantime, the rest of the day is mine."

They sat close together on the sun-warmed sand, moving from time to time in an effort to keep in the shade. They didn't talk much, but Laura didn't mind that. It was heaven just to be close to him, his arms about her, her head on his hair-roughened chest. When the air began to cool with the approach of evening, Ahmed got to his feet, reaching down to pull her up against him.

"Come, my love," he said, his English only slightly edged with accent. "I have a table booked for seven-thirty at the Hilton, so I shall pick you up at seven o'clock."

Feeling in the same trance-like state, Laura showered and dressed with the utmost care. Her full-length dress of inca patterned silk in muted orange and brown looked perfect with her gleaming hair and sun-kissed skin. Glancing at the watch on her wrist, she knew that Ahmed would be on his way over to her. Knowing that they were to dine at his hotel, she had offered to take a cab over there, but he wouldn't hear of it. He had been quite adamant when she'd made the suggestion, telling her that he'd rather come for her himself. The members of the company would have already left for the theatre. Laura was glad about this. Not that she minded any of them seeing her with Ahmed. It was just that she didn't want to share him with anyone.

From time to time throughout the past hours while they'd been so close together, she had wanted to ask him about Françoise, but, fearing his reply, she preferred to torment herself in silent conjecture.

When the clerk on reception rang her room to tell her that Ahmed was waiting for her in the lounge, Laura took another hasty look at her reflexion in the full-length mirror. Satisfied with what she saw, she put all thought of Françoise from her mind and hurried out of the room to where Ahmed waited.

His look was tender as she walked towards him, the light brush of his fingers on her arm telling her more than mere words.

Once they were in the confines of the car his hand felt for hers and held on to it.

"It seems a lifetime since I last held you," he said.

"It's barely an hour since you left me at the hotel." She smiled up at him in the friendly darkness.

"I can't bear the pain of being away from you for half of that time," he said, lifting her fingers to his mouth.

The table he had reserved for their meal was well placed, not too near the centre of the dining room, not too far away from the raised dais where a small band played seductive background music for the diners.

"My uncle was delighted by your

gift." Ahmed mentioned the fact just after they had ordered their meal. "It was a good choice. Was it yours, or was it Steve's?"

"I chose it actually, but we were together the day I bought it."

"Does your heart still ache for him now that the engagement between you no longer exists?" he asked.

Looking up swiftly, she saw that his eyes were coldly mocking.

Her eyes widened with shock at the change in his mood.

"You look surprised, Laura. Surely you have been informed that Steve is soon to marry with that young nurse of his."

"Of course I knew that was what Steve hoped for, but as yet I haven't heard from him about it."

"The news does not distress you, then?" he asked, disbelief lending a curl to the corner of his mouth.

"Steve and I will always be friends, but we both realized that marriage to each other was not for us."

"But I thought, everyone thought, that he was the one who had managed to ease the pain for you after Omar."

"Steve understood about Omar; he understood me and so he gave me his friendship unstintingly. I'm happy for him and his Gloria. He's a darling, and I hope he will find happiness this time."

His hand reached for hers as it rested on the table across from him.

The waiter chose that precise moment to bring the first course of their meal, and so Ahmed let go of Laura's hand. No sooner had he left their table when the fingers gripped her hand again.

"So your heart is free once more?" he said, his voice low in the back of his throat.

"I have no commitments, legal or otherwise," Laura replied.

"Will you be my wife, Habeeba?" he asked, lifting her hand until it reached his mouth.

Laura tried to answer him but couldn't.

"Well, my love, what is your answer? You wouldn't say no to me, would you?"

"I might," she replied, needing to play for time.

"I know you care for me, and you know how much I've wanted you since that very first day when I followed you to Leptis."

About to mention Françoise, she changed her mind because of the tender look that passed between them.

"Laura, I am not the kind of man to beg, but now I'm begging you to say yes to me."

She looked down at the soup before her on the table.

"I've never been proposed to over the first course of dinner, before." She gave him a tremulous smile.

He slid the heavy gold signet ring from his little finger and slid it onto the second finger of her left hand.

"Now we are betrothed. We shall marry the day after Suleiman makes Jameela his bride."

He picked up his spoon. "Come, eat, Habeeba, and we will talk afterwards."

"There can be no going back now, Laura," he said later, as they began the second course of the meal. "We belong to each other now and for always."

Laura just couldn't take it all in. Never, in all her wildest dreams, did she think that Ahmed would ask her to marry him.

"The men don't still have harems these days, do they?" she asked.

Ahmed shook his head, his eyes alight with laughter. "If there were harems, as in the bygone days, I should have no need of such a thing. With you to share my life, to share my loving, why should I need other women," he said matter-of-factly.

They were at the coffee stage when he gave her the envelopes from the inside pocket of his well-cut jacket.

"Better read the letters from the family." He smiled at her in the way that never failed to send the hot blood zipping along her veins. "After we have finished our coffee, I wish to dance with you. I haven't yet held you close to me with music playing in the background," he said, his dark eyes all but devouring her.

Laura read the letter from her father-in-law first. He thanked her for the thoughtful gesture of sending both the painting of Omar and the chess pieces. The letter closed on a hopeful note for the future. It seemed that they already knew of Ahmed's intentions towards her.

"You've already spoken to them about me?" She looked up with some surprise.

"How did they take it?" She asked when he told her that, yes, he had informed them.

"It was a foregone conclusion," he replied. "I have no secrets from the man who took me as his son. He knew how I felt about you, from the start."

The second letter was from Suleiman telling her how much he and Jameela were looking forward to seeing her again. Opening the last of the three envelopes, Laura was surprised to see Françoise's signature at the bottom of the single sheet of writing paper.

"You will be surprised and happy to know that I am to marry with Paul, a fellow Frenchman, early next year," Françoise had written in her small, neat hand. "Be kind to my poor Ahmed," the letter continued. "He assures me that I have lost my senses. He will not understand that Paul has swept me off my feet."

Laura re-read the short letter, then folding it back into the envelope, she pushed all three of them into her small grosgrain evening bag.

"It seems that marriage is certainly in the air." She forced a smile to her lips. "Who is this Paul Françoise is engaged to? Has she known him long?" she asked carefully.

"He's an engineer, been working in Benghazi for a year or two," he replied. "She hasn't known him long and he's hardly the kind of man to make

Françoise happy. Still, she may come to her senses in time," he said, getting to his feet and reminding Laura that he was waiting to dance with her.

His arm was warm and firm across her back as they moved to the music. She knew he would be a good dancer. He had that animal grace about him, that easy way of moving even when he walked across a room.

When his hand moved down to the small of her back, urging her closer to him, her heartbeats quickened. She felt his warm breath stirring the soft tendrils of hair across her forehead, and wondered how she could still feel the same way about him, knowing, now, that he was only using her as a shield for his wounded pride. If only he had told her that Françoise had turned him down for this other man, she wouldn't have felt so hurt about it. She might even have agreed to go through with yet another make-believe engagement. Now the joy had gone from the day of exciting happenings, and her heart felt heavy in her breast.

He moved his lips gently against her cheek and whispered her name entreatingly. Her traitorous heart lightened in response, and looking up she met the dark eyes staring down into hers.

"Laura," he whispered again, "let us go from here. I can't bear to hold you like this with others looking on."

She felt him tremble against her and knew a swift feeling of elation. He might still want to marry Françoise, but if he was merely intending to bide his time until Françoise came to her senses, then this time he'd been hoist by his own petard. He'd asked her to marry him, and now she intended to make sure that he would keep his part of the bargain.

9

LAURA kept her chatter light and frivolous during the short journey back to her hotel. Ahmed seemed happy enough to keep it that way.

"What time will this Jim, the one you say is in charge of the theatre company, be back tonight?" he asked.

"Why do you want to know?" she asked, turning to look up at him in the dull light of the car's interior.

"I must explain that you will be leaving them after tomorrow. We go back to Tripoli the day afterwards."

"Ahmed. Be sensible," she said, trying to speak normally. "I can't just leave at such short notice."

"Are you telling me that you are not intending to come back with me?" He moved further away but continued to stare down at her.

"Let's wait until we get back to the hotel, then I'll try to explain why I can't go with you so soon."

There was no sign of any of the others in the lounge of the hotel as Laura walked beside Ahmed towards the lift area. Perhaps they'd all gone on for a drink somewhere after the performance was over.

As soon as they were inside her room, the door closed and the lights on, Ahmed stood in front of her, one hand resting lightly on the edge of the small table, the other pushed into the pocket of his black, narrow-legged trousers.

"Now. Explain to me why you cannot leave this travelling group of players to return home with me."

"I have commitments with the company. They need me until they get someone else to replace me," she replied, turning to put her evening bag onto the glass topped dressing table.

"I also need you, Laura. You've no idea how much."

Before she could frame a reply he reached for her, pulling her close against him. He'd unfastened his jacket, taken off his tie, and Laura felt the thudding of his heart through the thin silk of his shirt. She had intended to stay placid in his arms, but at the first touch of his lips against hers she was like a flame in the wind as his hand on her back arched her closer to him.

Thoughts of her loyalties to the company, his entanglement with Françoise were forgotten. All her high ideals were tossed away like a leaf on the autumn's breeze. She tried once, albeit half-heartedly, to push her hands against his chest. The buttons of his shirt gave way and her fingers felt the tangle of dark chest hair before she slid her hands up to rest them behind his head. She heard his swift, indrawn breath before he lifted her against him to carry her over towards the only bed in the room.

The coarse weave of the colourful bedspread was rough against her bare back, and Laura realized through the mists of desire that the long zip of her dress had opened. She couldn't recall Ahmed shedding his jacket or his shirt, but when he lowered himself on top of her, after flicking off the bright bedside light, her hands encountered the warm skin of his back. The longing to possess and be possessed was uppermost in Laura's mind as his hands and mouth trailed exciting arcs over her trembling body. She'd never felt such longing before, but just as he was about to take her it was as if some alarm bell triggered off in her mind.

"Ahmed. Please, please don't." Her words were low as she forced them from her throat — a throat that hurt now with the ache of unshed tears. But Ahmed heard the note of pleading, and with trembling self-control held her silently against him.

After a little while, he moved away from her, one hand still against her breast.

"You should have stopped me

before, my love," he said. "Forgive me for allowing my feeling to almost get the upper hand."

"There's nothing to forgive." She turned her head to smile at him in the semi-darkness. "The longing was the same for me."

He moved closer again, his hands gentle, his lips warm without the heat of passion.

"Perhaps it will be better if you don't come back with me the day after tomorrow."

Laura didn't know how to reply. She heard the hum of the night time traffic as it passed along the road beneath the window of her room, and watched the reflected light from the headlamps streaking across the darkened ceiling.

Had there been a note of relief in his voice? Had he been grateful to her for not encouraging him at that last moment? She felt him move away from her, and seconds later he was standing beside the bed looking down at her. Though the room was in comparative darkness, she crossed her hands self-consciously over her breasts. She caught the gleam of his teeth as he smiled down at her and then he reached for her hands.

"Don't cover yourself, Laura. You are quite safe, I assure you, but don't deny me the pleasure of looking at you. I must have something to keep me going until you come to me at the end of the time of Ramadan."

"You mean I am to come to you later?" she asked.

"It will be better, I think, if you stay away from me until almost the day set aside for our wedding. Otherwise I wouldn't be able to keep my hands off you."

"And what if I don't come to you?" she asked.

"Then I shall know that you don't want to be my wife, that you don't really feel the need to share my life, to take my loving."

"You won't come for me, then?"

"No. I won't come for you again.

The next time you must come to me, then I shall know that our coming together is a mutual thing."

He bent then to claim her lips once more before pulling her gently to her feet.

"It's too early to leave you, but you are too much of a temptation to stay alone with." He ran his fingertips down the curve of her cheek and down across the swell of her breasts. "How would you like to visit the casino? I'll stake you," he added, before she had the chance of wondering if she could afford it.

"I'd love to go with you," she said. "I've never been to a casino before."

It didn't take them long to get ready to go out again, and as they rode down in the lift together Ahmed told her how beautiful she looked.

Laura's heart was as light as thistledown for the remainder of the evening. The feeling of excitement that quickened her senses as she stepped into the brightly lit casino stayed with her until she was back in her own room at the hotel. Neither she nor Ahmed had won anything at the tables but that hadn't bothered either of them. Just being beside him, feeling the gentle touch of his fingers on her elbow or the warmth of his thigh as he'd stood behind her had been more exciting then having a winning streak.

Before Ahmed had left her at her hotel he'd asked her if she would meet him about eight o'clock. "We'll have breakfast together," he'd suggested. "Somewhere quiet, just the two of us, then I shall return to Tripoli by an earlier flight, now that you won't be accompanying me." His arms had reached for her. "And if you won't allow me to share your bed for what is left of the night," he'd said smiling tenderly down at her, "I think I shall deserve a further couple of hours of your company."

"What shall we do?" Laura had asked.

"Walk. Hold hands, touch as lovers

do." He'd laughed softly, kissing her once more before saying good night to her.

Sleep came easily to Laura. Her last thoughts before her eyelids closed were of the strong arms that had held her, the hands that had touched her with gentle expertize, and the small pleading cry that had stopped him from carrying her over the brink into paradise.

$$\star \quad \star \quad \star$$

Laura was ready and waiting in the foyer when Ahmed came for her. With his polaroid sunglasses, white T-shirt and the denim jeans he looked like any other tourist out for the day. Watching him as he walked towards her with that long-legged easy stride of his, Laura had difficulty stopping herself from running into his arms.

"You slept well, Habeeba?" His voice was deep in the back of his throat.

Laura felt suddenly tongue-tied but she managed to nod.

"Come then. We must not waste one minute of our time together," he said, taking hold of her arm.

The morning air held the promise of heat, and as they stepped out into the quiet street Laura tried to lengthen her stride to match his as he took her hand and moved towards the place where he wanted to eat breakfast. Later, sitting beneath the striped umbrella outside the white painted building with the pale blue shutters they made plans for their future.

"Shall I have to wait for a visa again?" Laura asked him.

"Everything has been taken care of. It seems your theatre group will be here for a further four weeks, so you will come to me when the rest of them return to London."

"How do you know how long we shall be in Malta? When did you see Jim?" she asked, a piece of bread half way up to her mouth.

"I telephoned him very early this morning," he told her.

"Good heavens. What did he say? Was he annoyed at being woken before mid-day?"

"He was very understanding once I'd explained everything. I am to meet with him before I leave for the airport. He wants to make certain that all is as it should be. He feels responsible for you, it seems."

"Jim's like that. You'll like him." She smiled across the table at him.

His hand reached out for hers.

"You have that special air about you which brings out the protective urge in all men," he said, carrying her fingers to his mouth.

"I shall miss you," he said softly as he turned her hand to kiss her palm. "Think about me often, mm?" he asked her, closing her fingers and placing her hand gently back onto the table.

"Every day," she promised him, lifting her hand again to touch the elongated mark that dimpled his lean cheek whenever he smiled.

"But what about the nights?" he said.

"That's when I shall ache for the warmth of you."

"The nights, too," she replied, feeling the hot colour sweeping up her cheeks.

They walked afterwards over rocks and boulders to a lonely spot with just water, winds and sky. They stood close together, the wind tugging at their hair, watching a huge flock of birds winging overhead.

"They are on the last part of their journeying," Ahmed told Laura. "Now that summer is giving way to the European autumn, the birds fly out to the warmth of my country's shores."

"Nature is fantastic," she breathed, moving closer to him. "How can so many birds find their way year after year without being shown the way? Perhaps news is passed down by word of beak or maybe they have built-in compasses."

"You'll find your way to me, my little dove." He turned her round to face him. "I will try to be patient until you fly into my arms."

"Will you be like the hawk looking down from your ancestral eyrie?"

Suddenly Laura recalled something Steve had once said to her, something about the hawk not mating with the dove. Without warning she started to shiver and buried her head against his chest. Did lightning strike twice? Fate couldn't take Ahmed from her in the same way as Omar had been taken. This time it was different. She loved Ahmed, she'd only cared for his younger cousin, but it had hurt her just the same.

"I've changed my mind." She looked up into his face. "I'll come back with you to Tripoli today. Don't leave me behind. I couldn't bear it."

His hands moved soothingly over her shoulders. "Don't worry, little one. I will take care," he said, knowing her thoughts instinctively.

He cradled her head against his chest until he felt the tension leave her, and then he kissed her and it felt to Laura as if they stood alone at the start of a brand new world.

She almost told him then that she loved him, the words trembling on her mouth to be bitten hastily back. He hadn't spoken to her of love, only that he wanted her, needed her. It wouldn't do to be the first to declare herself. After all, this could be merely an interval in time, a time of waiting for Françoise to come to her senses, as he'd called it.

"Better now?" he asked, bending his head to rest his lips against each of her closed eyelids. Tasting the salt of her tears he rocked her gently to and fro, patting her back like one would do to a child.

"Yes. Yes. I'm all right now." She opened her eyes to look up at him. "Forgive me for spoiling our time together."

"I, too, could weep at the thought of leaving you behind, but time will pass, even though it will be slowly." He gave her a heart-rending smile. "Come, let us see how quickly we can reach the town."

They had lunch with Jim, who insisted on knowing their future plans.

"I'm a grown woman, Jim," Laura told him, while Ahmed went to make a phone call. "There isn't any need to keep asking questions."

"I just had to make sure, girlie. I'm satisfied now." He patted her hand. "But, to be honest, I wouldn't have been much of a compatriot if I hadn't made certain that all was as it should be."

When it was time for Ahmed to leave, Jim insisted upon taking him out to the airport.

"Now, you are certain you have all our plans fixed firmly in your head?" Ahmed asked Laura, as they sat together in the back seat of Jim's hired car.

"Yes. I know them all back to front," she assured him.

"Your ticket, etcetera, will be delivered to you within the next day or so," he told her. "I'll meet you when you get in, so don't worry about a thing."

Reaching the airport, Jim said he would wait in the car for Laura.

"Take your time, love," he told her. "I've got plenty of time."

After Ahmed had checked in his luggage at the desk he led her over to a secluded corner. Taking hold of her hand he removed his signet ring from her finger and slid another one in its place.

"The fit is perfect," he said. "This was my mother's and her mother's before that. I hope you like it."

Laura looked down at the heavy gold ring with the clustered wine-red stones.

"It's beautiful," she breathed. "But where did you get it from?"

"I took it out of my safe when I decided to visit you," he told her.

"You were so certain that I would agree to marry you, then?"

"As sure as winter comes before spring," he assured her.

"I've never known a man with such

conceit," she said, and meant it.

She felt the need to get away from him. Making the excuse of not wanting to see him leave, she said that she wanted to go.

"You don't mind, do you?" she asked.

"Not at all, my dove. I have some papers I can study."

He'd never been one for kissing or holding her in public, so she wasn't perturbed when he merely shook hands and then kissed her on both cheeks.

"Until we meet again," he said, staring deeply down at her.

"Goodbye," she whispered, turning away swiftly in case he should notice the tears that weren't far away.

She didn't turn to look back, but hurried out to where Jim waited.

Now that Ahmed wasn't beside her Laura found it easier to think. Over the next few days she might be able to sort out her jumbled emotions. It would be good to get back to work, to build up her strength, as it were, ready for the time when Ahmed should ask her to release him. When she was in bed at the end of the day she stared up into the darkness of her room, and relived the happenings of the past couple of days. It was on this bed that she had changed her mind about making her marriage to Ahmed a certainty. She knew that once he'd taken her he wouldn't have backed out of the engagement, even if Françoise had been free. Being a man of his word, such an action would have been unthinkable. By asking him not to, she had made it possible for him to be released honourably. The engagement ring that he'd slid on to her finger, in the secluded spot in the otherwise crowded airport, felt heavy on her slender hand. She thought about the two other women who had also worn the ring in their life time, and wondered what each of them would have done had they been in similar circumstances. Would either of them have returned the ring without being asked, losing Ahmed but keeping pride, or would they have made themselves indispensable to him, making his other love seem mediocre?

What was it Ahmed had said to her? Something about belonging to him even though they were not yet legally bound to each other. Well, he belonged to her in just the same way. What she had, she would hold. Françoise had had her chance and turned it down, so that was that. She, Laura, would marry Ahmed. She would love him, cherish him, until the end of time and Ahmed, being an honourable man, would forsake Françoise or any other woman in his life.

When Laura went back to work after the weekend she told the ones who didn't already know that she would be leaving them.

"Will you fit in with the Libyan way of life?" Peter wanted to know.

"I'm sure I will," Laura smiled in reply.

"He's a good looking guy if he's the

one I saw you walking away from the hotel with, early the other morning." Lesley looked up from the velvet costume she was busily mending.

"Looked a bit fierce to me," Anita said. "I only hope you know what you're doing, Laura."

"You've no need to worry, honestly," Laura assured her new found friends. "They are all lovely people and I adore the country, even the heat."

Throughout the next couple of weeks Jim also asked Laura if she was still certain that she wanted to go through with her marriage to Ahmed. "Once we leave Malta for home, the chance to come back with us will be lost," he reminded her. "Though, if you do change your mind at a later date, there will be nothing to stop you getting back to the UK."

Laura thanked him for his concern but assured him that everything was just as she wanted it.

Deciding to spend on clothes most of the wages Jim gave her, she asked

Anita, Karen and Tanya if they would like to go with her to the shops. Lesley and Vidette had already gone off together, otherwise Laura would have liked them all to be with her. She particularly wanted to buy something to wear for the wedding of Suleiman and Jameela.

"What about your own wedding? What kind of outfit are you going to wear?" Karen asked, as they browsed around the well stocked shops.

"A dress, I think. Something long, but nothing too fancy, if you know what I mean."

After a while, feeling spoilt for choice, Laura finally decided on a smart little dress and jacket in soft aqua green. "This will be fine," she said as she looked at her reflexion in the full-length mirror in the fitting room. "It won't need shortening if I wear my high-heeled sandals."

It was just as they were walking out of the shop that Laura saw the cream silk dress in the showcase.

"It's beautiful, but I bet it will cost the earth," Anita said when Laura pointed it out to them.

"I don't care what it costs. If it's the right size, I shall have it," she said rashly.

The size was right, so was the price. Breathing a sigh of relief because of the latter, Laura slid the pale silken creation over her head and knew that she'd found the right dress for her own special day. Because she'd been married before, she knew she wouldn't have to go through the extensive ceremonies that Jameela would have to go through. She and Ahmed would no doubt be married at the British Embassy. Just a quiet affair with none of the usual feasting and fairy lights of the traditional Arabic wedding.

The month had flown away, but the last couple of days seemed to drag. Her flight was to leave Malta a couple of hours after the others were due to depart.

"Don't let that worry you," she said

to Jim when he mentioned this to her. "After you've gone I shall pass the time in the restaurant."

She didn't feel at all lonely after the others had actually left the airport. She was glad really of having this chance of being alone. It would give her the chance of getting her thoughts in order.

She wondered if Ahmed was feeling as churned up inside as she was. She felt suddenly shy of meeting him, and foolishly began to hope that the plane would be unavoidably delayed. But right on time the flight was called, and Laura followed the other passengers through the departure gate. The journey seemed shorter even than last time. In no time at all Laura was looking down at the bright blue waters of the harbour stretched out beneath them.

Once they'd landed and reached the airport buildings, Laura had her emotions well under control. Straightening the slim fitting skirt of her smart navy-blue suit as she waited in line at the customs check point, she wondered if Ahmed was even now waiting for her at the other side of the barriers. At last she was free to go, and her heart's pace accelerated in sweet anticipation.

Carrying her case and matching flight bag, Laura followed one of the other passengers from the same flight as herself, out into the large reception area. Her excited gaze passed over the people waiting there, searching for the familiar tall, broad-shouldered figure. Ahmed wasn't there. Had he been delayed? Hearing her name she turned swiftly to find Françoise walking towards her. With legs that felt as if they'd lost all strength Laura crossed the five or so yards separating her from the French girl.

"Is Ahmed . . . ill?" she asked, anxiety clouding her brow.

"Of course not," Françoise replied breezily. "He's never ill. You should know that. He just asked me to pick you up. That is all."

It was with great difficulty that Laura

maintained her air of quiet calm as she walked with Françoise to where the car was parked. Once inside the vehicle she wanted to ask the other girl if her engagement to the young engineer was still on, but, deciding against this, she asked instead about different members of the family, while Françoise handled the big car with practised ease as they moved at speed away from the airport.

"Are you intending to stay on at the villa after the wedding of Suleiman and Jameela?" the French girl asked, without taking her eyes from the road.

Laura turned her head in surprise. Hadn't Ahmed mentioned anything about their future? Had he in fact . . . changed his mind?

"I'm . . . not quite sure," she replied, deciding to compromise a little.

With the tip of her thumb she touched the edge of the ring Ahmed had slid onto her finger a little over a month ago. She decided to remove it at the first opportunity, especially before Françoise should notice and pass comment about it. Her chance came when the other girl pulled into the side of the road and stopped the car.

"I'm just going to get some bananas," she said, getting from the car and walking the few yards back to the roadside stall.

Laura watched her for a second or two before slipping the ring from her finger and placing it in the safest part of her bag.

"I like bananas when they are a bit green like this." Françoise got back into the car and deposited onto the back seat the plastic bag full of the fruit she had purchased.

"How is your work at the clinic? Are you very busy there?" Laura asked once they were on the way again.

"It is always busy there. I shan't be sorry to leave."

"You aren't intending to carry on working after you are married, then?" Laura asked.

"That, my marriage, won't be taking place for ages. I have decided to take

Ahmed's advice to wait awhile. Perhaps I was a little, how do you say, impetuous." She grinned with that gamine charm of hers. "I am leaving the clinic, though. I shall go back to France for a while, once all the fuss and excitement of Jameela's wedding is over."

"What will you do then? When you come back, I mean?" Laura tried to speak evenly but even to her own ears the words had a breathless sound to them.

"Stay at the villa to be company for my aunt. At least, that is what my uncle would like me to do," Françoise replied. She told Laura then, in her attractively accented voice, that although she always referred to the Saheeds as her aunt and uncle, they were only slightly related on the female side of the family.

Laura recognized familiar landmarks, and knew that they were nearing the villa. How would Ahmed greet her, and how would she greet him? She tried to plan some sort of conversation, keeping everything light and easy between them. She could mention the flight out from Malta, and anything about the last couple of weeks with the theatre lot. They had to stop at the crossroads, and as they waited for the traffic to start moving again Laura noted the way Françoise's fingers were beating an impatient tattoo on the steering wheel. Was she annoyed at having to wait for the lights or was she agitated on some other account? The lights changed and the car shot forward, nosing its way into lane as Françoise cut the corner. The fingers still tapped the wheel and a little of her agitation communicated itself to Laura. She couldn't wait now to get to the villa.

It was something of an anti-climax, however, to find when she got there that Ahmed was away from the home. The older members of the family greeted her with a warmth that had been sadly missing on that other, earlier visit to their home. Even the old aunts held their arms out to her, clasping her in turn to their bony chests.

"When will Ahmed be back?" Laura asked Mr Saheed, at the first opportunity that presented itself.

"He was called out early this morning," the old man explained, "and will not be back until tomorrow."

Laura wished then that she hadn't bothered coming out to Tripoli. She should have gone back home with the others. At least she had known where she stood with them. With Ahmed, it had always been a case of blow hot, blow cold. Thinking about the time when she'd first visited Tripoli she recalled Ahmed's aloof manner towards her. In those days she'd made no secret of his dislike of her. And afterwards, when she'd known that he was attracted to her, there had still been times when he'd looked at her with cold indifference. Had he been merely baiting her during that magical time in Malta? Had it been his way of making sure that she was present at the wedding of his other, younger cousin? Was it, in fact, his way of punishing her for marrying Omar in the first place? Had he, like the others, blamed her for Omar's untimely death? Laura shivered in spite of the heat of her room. Crossing to the window she opened wide the casement. The familiar sharp, sweet smell of citrus swept inwards on the warm breeze. Looking out, down onto the well-tended garden, she watched the silvery feathered doves floating down to the ornate dove-cote under the eucalyptus trees. Tea was brought up to her room by the same serving girl who'd looked after her on her last visit, but when it was time to go with the womenfolk to one of the celebrations to do with Jameela's wedding, she pleaded a head-ache and asked to be excused. The headache that had been merely a make-believe thing became a fact before the misty cloak of evening fell, and Laura was glad then just to crawl into bed. The next day was to be the big feast day, the day when Suleiman and

Jameela would be actually married. She'd have to be fresh to attend. A headache would be no excuse. She'd have to marshal every bit of pride she could. Neither Ahmed nor the rest of the family would find her wanting.

Laura had breakfast in her room. Afterwards she showered, washed and blow-dried her hair, and then dressed carefully for the day's celebrations. She was pleased with the result as she took a last look in the long mirror before going down to join Omar's mother and the two elderly aunts. Apparently they weren't to travel in the same car as the men, and for this small thing Laura was grateful. The longer she put off meeting Ahmed again, the better equipped she'd be. Or so she told herself. Was he back from wherever he'd been to? Was he indeed on his way to the ceremony right now, with Françoise as his partner? Surely he wouldn't humiliate her in such a fashion. He wouldn't do that to her, she knew that. It was all one big mix up. Once the day's celebrations were over, she'd make for the airport. This time she had her passport safe in her own handbag.

The huge tent in the grounds of Jameela's father's villa was bedecked as usual with fairylights, their glow ineffectual in the bright light of day. The inside of the tent was crowded to capacity, and, feeling herself observed, Laura looked up to find Ahmed staring across at her. His glance was cold, as it had been in the past, and Laura felt as if the world had exploded, leaving her feeling in need of air. Looking swiftly to right and left she turned on her heel and made for the wide entrance. Suleiman and Jameela detained her just as she was about to leave the tent.

"Laura," Jameela's small hand settled on her arm, "they told me you were here, but it seemed too good to be true."

How could she push by the radiant bride and her darkly handsome groom?

"I'm happy to be here," she lied. "You look beautiful, Jameela, and I hope you'll both be very happy," she said, and meant every word of it.

At that moment Ahmed came up from behind her. She knew he was there even before he spoke.

"Didn't I tell you, Laura, that it is no use trying to run away from me?" he said, his hand light upon her shoulder.

Laura turned her head to look up at him, surprised at the anger smouldering down at her from his narrowed gaze.

"I was trying to get out for air," she said truthfully, as someone else distracted the happy couple's attention.

"Come, then. I will escort you," he said, manoeuvring her through the crowd. Just as she was about to walk out into the fresh air she turned her head and saw Françoise resplendent in bright, emerald green. She was standing with a tall, rangy young man with auburn, curly hair. So that must be Paul, she mused. He must be the reason Ahmed had come to her.

"I'm quite capable of going by myself," she reminded Ahmed. "In fact

I'd rather be alone."

He ignored her words, taking her arm until they were outside the tent.

"Your days of being alone are over. Or have you forgotten that tomorrow you will be Mrs Saheed, for the second time around."

"There's no need to be unkind about it, Ahmed. Besides, I've changed my mind. I won't be getting married tomorrow."

"You will keep your word, Laura," he said in that deep voice of his that never failed to stir her senses. "It is time you looked the truth in the face, time you steered the straight path instead of wanting to dash from one side to the other."

"And what of you, Ahmed? Will you have the strength to keep to the one path without feeling the need to look back?"

The way he looked at her was almost pleading.

"I will make you forget everything from your past, and you in turn will make certain I don't remember anything but the life we have together," he said in that arrogant way of his. "Now come, let us go back inside or they will all think that you've abducted me."

The smile he gave her was her undoing and she turned to walk beside him. The meal was almost ready to begin and Laura felt a blush teasing up her cheeks as everyone seemed to be looking in their direction.

It was after midnight when Laura and Ahmed left the celebration tent. She hadn't expected to be able to stay behind after Omar's mother and father had left with the two aunts. When she'd got up to leave when they did, Ahmed had placed a restraining hand on her arm.

"Your days of leaving without me are over," he'd said, his voice a husky whisper against her cheek.

Now they were in the car, Ahmed's cloak thrown carelessly behind onto the back seat.

"Shall we drive along the coast road

until we see the dawn rise?" he said, setting the vehicle in motion.

"Yes. Yes, if you like," she replied, anxious to keep this near-to-loving feeling between them. He'd been gentle in his manner towards Françoise when she'd walked across the tent to speak to them after the meal had been cleared away. His manner to Paul, on the other hand, had been faintly hostile. Laura decided to push all thoughts of Françoise to the back of her mind. She'd taught herself over the past months to switch off, to discard unwanted thoughts. If she wanted to make a good life with Ahmed, then she'd have to be firm in her resolve. There would be no room for uncertainty or petty jealousy. She'd just have to pretend that Françoise didn't exist, as far as Ahmed was concerned, anyway.

They travelled along the bright ribbon of road, with neither of them seeming inclined to talk. Laura didn't mind that. Her thoughts were too full of things that could be spoilt by a careless word.

It was Ahmed who eventually broke the silence.

"Have you lost the ring I gave you?" he asked, without taking his eyes from the road.

"No. It's in my bag," she replied.

"Well, put it back onto its proper place," he said, slowing down to pull off the road. They weren't far from the sea. Laura could hear it as it pounded against the shore, reminding her of the noise she'd heard in shells pressed against her ear in those happy, far off days of childhood.

"Why do you hesitate?" he asked, getting from the car and moving round to open the door for her.

The moon was high above them as they stood together in the darkness. "Well," he prompted, taking her arm as they walked from the car to where the road stopped and the shore began. The sand still retained the heat of the day as it seeped through the open strapwork of her sandals. "If you have misplaced the ring, say so, girl. I can always get you another one even though another would not have such sentimental value."

"The ring is in my bag. To be quite honest, I wasn't sure whether I was expected to wear it, or not."

"You can please yourself about wearing it, but our marriage takes place tomorrow with or without that particular ring being on your finger."

So they were still to be married, were they? Laura looked up at him.

They stopped walking just where the waves creamed up to the sand, darkening it and then receding.

"You haven't forgotten about tomorrow, have you?" he asked, without turning his head to look down at her.

"I wasn't quite sure whether . . . it was still on," she replied.

"You came willingly this time to my country, so it seems to me that you considered our betrothal to be valid."

Laura didn't know how to answer

him. It was on the tip of her tongue to tell him to go to Françoise, and be damned to the arrangements he'd made for the following day. Why should she be his second best? She was sick of having to dance to his tune.

The moon hid behind a cloud just as Ahmed's hands settled on her shoulder to turn her round to face him.

"Well. Are we to marry tomorrow, or not?" he asked, his face a pale blur in the darkness.

"Do the others know about your . . . our plans?" she asked.

"I didn't think it necessary to inform anyone. It is our business, yours and mine. Nothing to do with anyone else."

"But I thought you told me that Mr Saheed knew about us," she said.

"He does. But no one knows that we are to marry tomorrow, except the people at the Embassy."

"Who will be there, at the ceremony, I mean?"

"Just you and I and the official who is to legalize the proceedings. Is there need for anyone else to be present?" He moved her closer to him.

The way he whispered her name against her mouth was her undoing. She welcomed his kiss, opening her mouth at the pressure of his. It was no good trying to fight the feelings that just being with him provoked. At least he desired her, there was no denying that. And if that was to be her lot, then so be it. She knew in her heart of hearts that she would welcome anything that he could give her. To live without him wouldn't be living, and so she would be content to be his second best.

The moon came out again and the night became as light as day. Laura felt Ahmed's heart beating strongly against hers and his well muscled thigh heavily against her.

"Come, Habeeba. We must leave here before I lose my senses and take you on the cold, damp sand."

Before Laura had the chance to say anything, he swept her up into his arms and carried her back to the car. Settling her down he kept his arms about her.

"We shall be happy together, make no mistake about that, Laura, my love. With the chemistry that works between us we shall hit the heights a million times," he said, before kissing her on the mouth once more.

He was very quiet on the way back to the villa, but he lifted her hand to place it on his leg just above the knee, and then smiled swiftly down at her while waiting for the traffic lights to change.

The rest of the family were in bed when they reached the silent building. The shutters were lowered against the wind of the night, the lamplight gleaming across the inner courtyard.

"Shall we go together to our wedding or would you prefer that we meet there?" he asked.

"I'll meet you at the appointed place," she replied without lowering her eyes from the look in his. "Will you arrange for someone to drive me there?"

"Be at the side entrance, near the

dove-cote and Yussef will be there waiting for you at eleven o'clock."

He walked with her as far as the place where the wide stairway divided.

"After tonight we shall never be away from each other," he said, bending his head to lightly touch her mouth with his.

"But what about the times when you have to go away on business?"

"You will accompany me," he said. "You would not want me to leave you behind."

She wasn't quite sure whether the last sentence had been a question or a statement. Either way, she knew that she couldn't bear to be parted from him. Almost as if they were on the same wavelength, he said, "I know that after tomorrow I shall not want to leave you behind, even on the very shortest trip."

He kissed her again, his hands moving down the length of her back, moulding her closer to his body. He breathed her name, his lips moving gently against hers and it was as if they breathed of each other.

When his arms released her Laura moved against him.

"Hold me, Ahmed, just for a little while longer," she whispered, not wanting him to leave her.

"I'd hold you against me all night if you'd let me." His lips met hers again, warm and delightfully sensual as he bent to slide one arm beneath her knees to lift her closely up against him, taking the right-hand turn of the stairway.

10

THE cream silk dress looked decidedly bride-like, Laura decided. Picking up her perfume from the glass topped dressing table she unscrewed the top and sprayed a liberal jet over her hair and shoulders, knowing that a certain amount of the perfume would evaporate before she met up with Ahmed. Glancing at the watch on her wrist she felt her heart skip in her breast; it was almost time to go.

Perhaps she would hang on a little, she smiled secretly. After all, it was the accepted thing for the bride to keep the groom waiting. She watched the seconds creeping round the small face of her watch. If she went now, she would arrive five or six minutes late.

Yussef was waiting for her and Laura slid into the back seat of the car, giving him a conspiratorial smile. There had been no one to see her hurrying down the stairs at the side of the house; even Mr Saheed hadn't been in the study as she'd passed the window. The streets were crowded as was usual at that time in the morning, and once or twice Laura saw Yussef checking his watch with the clock on the dash. With fast beating heart she watched for familiar landmarks and knew that they were almost there. Yussef turned into a side street to park the car and then walked with her to the building where Ahmed would be waiting for her.

"We are a little late, Madam," Yussef looked decidedly worried.

"That's all right," she smiled in an effort to reassure him, "I will take the blame."

A doorkeeper opened the door for her with a flourish and looking into the high-ceilinged room Laura saw Ahmed talking to two men, one sitting, the other standing. He had his back to her and hearing the rustle of her dress he wheeled round to face her.

"You're late," he greeted her, running his finger along the inside edge of his collar.

"A lady's privilege," she reminded him, feeling a flicker of pleasure because of his discomfort.

The ceremony was brief, but Laura was sure that it was none the less binding. She felt suddenly shy of this tall, dark-haired man whose hand was warm on her elbow as they walked out into the bright sunlight together. She looked about for Yussef.

"He's driven back to the villa." Ahmed smiled down at her. "You didn't think I was going to allow him to take you back when I have my car here?" He lifted a dark winged brow as he opened the door of the car for her.

Last night he'd mentioned something about taking her away for a week or so, but he hadn't said where he intended taking her. Laura didn't mind, but didn't really want to spend the first few days of her married life with the others looking on, as it were.

"When do you intend to tell the family that we are now husband and wife?" she asked.

"I have no doubt that Yussef will have told them by now." He smiled indulgently down at her as he set the car in motion. "But we shall have no time to spend in explanations. As soon as we get to the villa, go to your room and change from this beautiful dress into something suitable for travelling."

About to ask him where they were going, he forestalled her, telling her that they would be travelling overland.

"I will send one of the girls up to help you to pack," he said, manoeuvring the big car with practised ease along the busy highway. "With luck we shall be ready to get off before midday."

"Won't the others expect us to spend a little while with them before we go dashing off?" she asked.

"Yussef will have the food basket and the cool drinks packed already for us, but we will stay just long enough to be courteous."

Feeling a little like a conspirator, Laura ran lightly up the side stairway when they arrived back at the villa. She had taken off her cream dress and was wearing a cool denim suit and cotton blouse when the girl arrived to help her to pack. Leaving her to finish putting the things into the two medium-sized cases, Laura ran lightly down the stairs into the inner courtyard.

The smile playing about her lips slipped when she saw the two people standing close together at the far end near to the tinkling fountain. They were so engrossed in what they were saying to each other that neither of them knew that Laura stood there, hand to mouth and feet rooted to the spot.

"The pain will pass, Françoise, believe me." Ahmed's deep toned voice reached Laura.

He had his back to her and when the French girl looked up at that moment Laura moved back into the shadow of the tall potted plant, not wanting either of them to see her standing there. The other girl said something to Ahmed and his arms reached out to enfold her. He kissed her once and then continued to hold her against him.

"Because of my foolish actions two people will spend their lives wishing things could have been different. But you understand how it was, don't you, Ahmed?"

It seemed to Laura that Ahmed was trying without much success to placate Françoise.

"This will be our secret, Ahmed. You promise." The girl's voice with its attractive accent lifted a little.

"Sh," the deeper voice cautioned her, "you don't want to alert the whole household, do you?"

"Promise me, then," Françoise continued to plead with him. "Not even Laura must be told. It is better that way, don't you agree?"

Laura didn't stop to wait for his reply. Skirting the potted palm she moved noiselessly out to the garden, fighting for composure as she moved towards the padded sun lounger.

It must have been quite a shock to Françoise to be told that Ahmed had married before her. According to the snatches of conversation she'd managed to pick up, Laura decided that Françoise was wishing now that she'd accepted Ahmed's proposal instead of deciding on Paul. Anger swept over Laura as she sat in the shade of the old eucalyptus. She wanted to run back inside, to rake her nails over the flawless beauty of the other girl's face, to pull the man's blue-black hair out by the roots, but common-sense prevailed. Nothing would be gained in the long run by such actions. Better to keep still and to take deep, even breaths of the citrus-spiked air until her heart stopped its wild pounding and her nerves settled down again.

At last she felt calm enough to go back inside. It would soon be time to leave on what she had looked upon earlier as the honeymoon. Thinking rationally, she decided that everything would be just as it was before she'd witnessed that touching little scene. Ahmed would never know that she'd watched and also overheard a little of their conversation. Given time, she might even forget it herself. Half of her wondered how she could be so stupid as to want to hang on to Ahmed. What had happened to the pride she'd always maintained was of such importance? Her other half whispered that pride would prove to be a cold bedfellow, and while ever she was with Ahmed, there was always the chance that he'd grow to love her as she loved him.

Ahmed watched her walking across the sun-warmed tiles of the courtyard and remembered that other time when he'd watched her walking over the same spot. He'd wanted her then, without knowing much about her. Now he knew everything and wanted her even more.

"Come, wife of mine. We must say goodbye to the family. They are waiting for you in the salon."

Feeling her slight recoil at his touch on her arm, he imagined her withdrawal to be for a different reason.

"There is no need for alarm, my love. My aunt and uncle are happy for us. Neither would have wished you to mourn their son for a life time. The older aunts are also pleased that I am to be your provider, your protector."

Only Françoise was absent as they walked into the large, sumptuously furnished room. When Laura asked about her, one of the aunts said that she was sulking in her room. The other informed her that tears had given the girl a headache and so she was lying down.

"No matter." Laura smiled gently from one to the other. "Tell her that I asked about her and that I hope the hurt will go away."

Laura looked up at Ahmed as she spoke but his expression didn't alter

247

one way or the other.

At last they were on the way, their luggage packed into the back of the Range Rover.

"You look a little jaded, Laura. Aren't you feeling well?" Ahmed asked when they'd been on the road for an hour or so.

"I've got a bit of a headache," she replied, and with some surprise found it was true.

"We'll pull up for a cool drink in a little while." He smiled, laughter lines crinkling the corners of his eyes.

He told her then that he had booked a room at a small hotel for the night. "You shall rest tonight, Habeeba. Tomorrow we will journey into the desert and when darkness sweeps across the sand, our life together will begin."

So the 'honeymoon' wasn't to start that night. Laura didn't know whether to laugh or cry. Perhaps the parting from Françoise had been too painful for him, she decided. Perhaps it would smack at mockery if he should desire his wife after saying goodbye to the other woman all in the same day.

In the end Laura was glad to tumble into the softness of the hotel bed, and to hear Ahmed saying good night to her falling asleep just as soon as her head touched the pillow. She didn't even hear the door shut behind him; didn't realize that he hadn't shared her room, let alone her bed, until she got up the following morning.

"You look better this morning, little one." He reached over to touch her cheek.

They were sitting at the breakfast table, the only two people in the small dining room.

It was still early when they resumed their journey. They were to rest during the hottest part of the day, and with luck would reach their destination well before evening.

"Are we going to the oasis, the place where we all stayed before?" she asked.

"No," he told her. "You were with

friend Steve on that occasion."

"And you were with Françoise," she reminded him.

The heat haze shimmered along the road, the scenery seeming to change with every mile. Buildings became scarce and the orange groves petered out until there was just the odd tree, the few clumped bushed dotted across the landscape. The solid road changed without warning and the Land Rover's wheels moved silently over the hoof marks left by camels that had recently passed that way.

"This is the true desert, but if you are not happy being here, just tell me and we will leave immediately," he said, stopping the vehicle beneath an untidy group of dusty palms.

About to recite the passage from the Scriptures about 'where thou goest, I will go,' she remembered that he had a different religion to hers. There were other reasons that could make their life together a difficult one. Their cultures were different.

When she mentioned this a moment or two later, he laughed at her. "You will not find me trying to convert you to the Islamic faith, any more than you would try to impose your beliefs on me. As for the culture, I could remind you that Libyans walked in marble halls while the ancient Britons shivered in caves."

"You told me that your forebears were the Tuareg who roamed the Southern Desert," she said.

"Tuaregs, Libyans, Britons, Romans, what do any of them matter to us? We are only people, after all." He reached for her hand and held it.

"You must tell me all about your people who are now my people," she said, feeling strangely at peace with this man who had seemed like a stranger since she'd watched him with Françoise a little more than twenty-four hours ago.

Ahmed flicked open the door.

"Come, my new bride, watch me pitch the tent that will be our home for the next few days."

His mood was light-hearted. He apparently had no hang-ups about Françoise. A case perhaps of 'out of sight, out of mind': she silently coined the phrase.

When he'd mentioned the tent, Laura had imagined it would be one of those bright orange and blue frame tents that she'd seen in the fields back home at holiday times but the one he took from the back of the Rover was made from the traditional dried camel skins like the one she'd shared with Françoise at the oasis.

"This will keep out the glare of the sun by day and the cold winds of night," Ahmed said, pulling the ropes that secured it. "You will have no need to fear the creepy-crawlies that always make the women scream." He turned to smile over his shoulder at her. "The ground sheet is boxed well up the sides, but I am afraid we have no carpet for the floor."

By this time he had taken off his

shirt, and Laura found a sensual delight in watching his well-muscled body as he worked. He had pumped up the large inflatable mattress and placed it along the far side of the tent.

"You can make up the bed and hang our clothes along the line over there," he said, "while I start cooking our evening meal."

He explained that they would be cooking on a portable Calor gas stove. "We are, how do you say, cheating a little bit." He laughed, that deep sound in his throat that never failed to set her nerve ends tingling with excitement.

Laura changed into a loose cotton jellaba and Ahmed shrugged his shoulders into a black, light-weight pullover.

The meal of canned meat, vegetables and macaroni tasted delicious.

"My compliments to the chef." Laura smiled at him as they sat cross-legged across from each other.

"More cheating, I'm afraid. Canned meat and vegetables and eaten with knives and forks." He ruffled her hair before taking her empty plate from her.

"How long will our water last?" she asked, as she watched him wash the dishes.

"Longer, I dare say, if I do the washing up, he replied, putting the equipment back into the back of the vehicle.

Just before darkness fell Ahmed lit a small fire in the clearing near to the front of the tent. "I love the smell of wood smoke," he said. "It reminds me of my childhood days."

"Won't the fire attract marauding tribesmen?" she asked, standing beside him.

"No one will harm you while I'm around," he said. "I have a gun if one should be needed, but there is no need to worry. We are as safe here as in the cities of the civilized world."

She could have told him that she didn't mind if the world came to an end, just as long as she was with him, but she didn't say anything.

In the far distance she saw bright orange balls of flame. Before she had the chance to ask Ahmed what they were, he explained that it was the ignited gas from the refinery-plant many, many miles away.

"We aren't near the plants or the pipe line, then?"

Ahmed shook his head. "I told you once before that it is forbidden to travel anywhere near there unless it is on company business. We are alone except for the stars and the moon that will soon be shining down upon us."

Laura lifted her head to look up at the stars pricking through the canopy of night. The cool wind lifted her hair and teased the hemline of her jellaba. She heard the cry of some small night creature, and moved instinctively nearer to her husband. It was strange to think of him in that term, and yet they were man and wife. She had the certificate in her bag to prove it.

"What is it, Laura? What is it that you have to say to me?"

"Perhaps I should ask you the same thing," she replied, playing for time.

He looked down at her in the darkness that enfolded them.

"For the first time in my life I feel out of my depth. I know what I want to say, but am not quite certain how to say it," he said laughing self-consciously.

"Why not start at the beginning. That is the usual place," she replied with a calmness she was far from feeling.

"From that very first time I saw you, I wanted you for my own," he began at last. "I was ashamed then, because Omar was still alive. Afterwards, when I should have been sharing your grief, you evoked feelings in me that I didn't want to feel." He stopped talking to rake his fingers through his hair.

"Yes," she prompted him. "Isn't there something else?"

"Oh, God, Laura. You don't want me to say anything else, do you?" He turned her face with his fingertips until she was looking up at him.

"Yes. It is only fair that I should know what you wish to keep from me," she said, bracing herself for the mention of Françoise's name.

"I was jealous of my dead cousin, and when I knew for certain that you and he had never . . . you know . . . made love together, I was happy for me, sad for Omar."

Was this the polished, well travelled Ahmed Saheed talking? She stared up at the pale blue of his face, and lifted her hand to touch the elongated scar along his cheek.

"And what of Françoise?" she asked. "Where does she fit into all this?"

"How do you mean? How can she fit into our lives?"

"I saw you together yesterday, after we got back from the Embassy. I also overheard what was being said between you." She felt relieved now that it was out in the open. "I suppose she had broken off with Paul, but broken it off too late," she said.

"No. Their arrangements still stand,

257

but she told Paul's sister that her husband had tried to flirt with her, and now that couple are . . . estranged. She, Françoise, wanted my reassurance, that is all."

"Yet you kissed her. I saw you," she continued.

"Wouldn't you kiss a distressed child if she asked you to?" He took hold of her hand and carried it to his mouth.

Laura felt her heart trip in her breast as his arms slid down to hold her close against him.

His lips were warm when they teased, light as thistledown, across hers.

"Laura," he whispered, without lifting his mouth from hers. "The time for talking is over. Tonight we share our loving."

THE END

*Other titles in the
Linford Romance Library:*

A YOUNG MAN'S FANCY
Nancy Bell

Six people get together for reasons of their own, and the result is one of misunderstanding, suspicion and mounting tension.

THE WISDOM OF LOVE
Janey Blair

Barbie meets Louis and receives flattering proposals, but her reawakened affection for Jonah develops into an overwhelming passion.

MIRAGE IN THE MOONLIGHT
Mandy Brown

En route to an island to be secretary to a multi-millionaire, Heather's stubborn loyalty to her former flatmate plunges her into a grim hazard.

WITH SOMEBODY ELSE
Theresa Charles

Rosamond sets off for Cornwall with Hugo to meet his family, blissfully unaware of the shocks in store for her.

A SUMMER FOR STRANGERS
Claire Hamilton

Because she had lost her job, her flat and she had no money, Tabitha agreed to pose as Adam's future wife although she believed the scheme to be deceitful and cruel.

VILLA OF SINGING WATER
Angela Petron

The disquieting incidents that occurred at the Vatican and the Colosseum did not trouble Jan at first, but then they became increasingly unpleasant and alarming.

DOCTOR NAPIER'S NURSE
Pauline Ash

When cousins Midge and Derry are entered as probationer nurses on the same day but at different hospitals they agree to exchange identities.

A GIRL LIKE JULIE
Louise Ellis

Caroline absolutely adored Hugh Barrington, but then Julie Crane came into their lives. Julie was the kind of girl who attracts men without even trying.

COUNTRY DOCTOR
Paula Lindsay

When Evan Richmond bought a practice in a remote country village he did not realise that a casual encounter would lead to the loss of his heart.

ENCORE
Helga Moray

Craig and Janet realise that their true happiness lies with each other, but it is only under traumatic circumstances that they can be reunited.

NICOLETTE
Ivy Preston

When Grant Alston came back into her life, Nicolette was faced with a dilemma. Should she follow the path of duty or the path of love?

THE GOLDEN PUMA
Margaret Way

Catherine's time was spent looking after her father's Queensland farm. But what life was there without David, who wasn't interested in her?

HOSPITAL BY THE LAKE
Anne Durham

Nurse Marguerite Ingleby was always ready to become personally involved with her patients, to the despair of Brian Field, the Senior Surgical Registrar, who loved her.

VALLEY OF CONFLICT
David Farrell

Isolated in a hostel in the French Alps, Ann Russell sees her fiancé being seduced by a young girl. Then comes the avalanche that imperils their lives.

NURSE'S CHOICE
Peggy Gaddis

A proposal of marriage from the incredibly handsome and wealthy Reagan was enough to upset any girl — and Brooke Martin was no exception.

A DANGEROUS MAN
Anne Goring

Photographer Polly Burton was on safari in Mombasa when she met enigmatic Leon Hammond. But unpredictability was the name of the game where Leon was concerned.

PRECIOUS INHERITANCE
Joan Moules

Karen's new life working for an authoress took her from Sussex to a foreign airstrip and a kidnapping; to a real life adventure as gripping as any in the books she typed.

VISION OF LOVE
Grace Richmond

When Kathy takes over the rundown country kennels she finds Alec Stinton, a local vet, very helpful. But their friendship arouses bitter jealousy and a tragedy seems inevitable.